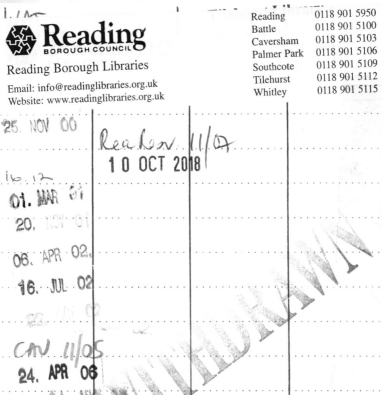

ABOUT THE AUTHOR

William Mayne set out to write books at the age of eight, and about twenty years later won the Carnegie Medal. By the millennium he will have had about a hundred in print, but he still thinks he works very slowly and spends whole days looking out of the window not doing the gardening and pretending he is thinking. When it is dark he gets out the ink and writes words down until they make sense. He thinks you don't get much done if you are busy.

Candlefasts follows on from *Cradlefasts* and *Earthfasts*. All three books are set in the part of Yorkshire where the author has lived for many years.

William Mayne

Candlefasts

William Mayne

Hodder
Children's
Books

a division of Hodder Headline

This is for Beth Relton

INGATES

ONE

The Surgery
Garebrough

To Sister Jeannie Mackenzie

Dear Jeannie,

You won't think well of me for not telling you anything, but we don't seem to be letter-writers, and busy with one thing and another I lost your address, and couldn't recall whether you were nursing in Muscat or St Helena, and I'm surprised to hear it was Montreal, and now back home again in bonny Scotland.

One of the busy things was moving house, because I now have a live-in position at the present address above. In fact, I married the doctor I work for, quite suddenly and unexpectedly. Now I can't find everything or anything from my old house, including letters and addresses. If you'd been a patient I was writing to I would know exactly where to find it all, and give you an appointment, because I am still efficient that way.

But we are so busy, two housefuls of furniture in one not very big house, and a lot of stuff put away in a building for the time being, because he, Ricky, is to retire from being the local medic next year but go on working by running nursing homes, because we're young to stop work. We are to live at a house called Crackpot Hall, very haunted and distant, miles from anywhere by English standards, up beyond Gunthwait, frayed at the edges and the roof fallen in – he has had his eye on it for years but didn't think he ought to live there.

Well, he's your brother-in-law, Richard, very cuddly of course, and funny (so you know it's serious). We are each other's belongings. You are an auntie, because Ricky was a widower with a son of about sixteen, David. Someone will find him cuddly one day, but for now he is leaping about and going to school, and totally in love with another woman, which makes me a wee bit jealous – I'll tell you how and why when I've said some more about him.

I was here in Garebrough, working at the Monks' Infirmary, when I first knew Ricky. I was a bit shy of getting close to him for two reasons. I'll explain more about one of them later, but the other reason was his son and what happened to him. I wanted to get out of hospital nursing, so I took the nurse's job at the surgery. I thought it would be easier, but not long after I began working there I began to want to manage his kitchen, and get the pair of them a wee bit of cooking done (they hadn't any idea) and so on, and it grew from there (sharing the washing up and so on).

But I should talk about the son David, and the weird time he had not long since. The whole town had heard about it, and wondered about the reality of it all, because such things don't happen these days. I'll explain.

~~Apparently~~ No, in fact, because it is undoubtedly true, tho' hard to fathom, actually. Actually, a year or two ago David was struck by a black lightning flash on the moors here, and seemed to be vaporised. His friend Keith saw it happen, and a local farmer, and a hiker. David was presumed dead at an inquest, because there was no trace of him, only for him to walk home a few months later. His friend found him up in the hills, together with a stot-herd called Nellie Jack John from the back of beyond and they do say another time altogether (of course, this ought to be fancy), some of them cut about and bleeding, and they made their way back. Ricky found them in his bathroom and doctored them up. It's what he does by nature, as well as being a dear man. But here I am, living in the house where it happened, using the bathroom where they all appeared (they found each other in a cave on the hillside somewhere, but they bled in the bathroom), and not hearing much more about the matter. It can't be explained, so it's being forgotten about, and I don't like to ask.

It would be psychological if it hadn't really happened, but there's no doubt it did. Of course it left a question over David, as if there was something wrong with him. There isn't, and it's obvious there isn't, when you get to know him. I don't enquire about it, because of not wanting to be inquisitive and speiring and it sounds like morbid curiosity. David can't remember what became of him for more than four months that winter. His diary goes until October, he says, and starts again in February, and he knows nothing between, except a feeling that one day he will remember. Also, the poor laddie was half orphaned when he was eight, and I knew his mother for she was my patient, who died in the Monks' Hospital, and her wee baby girl was dead too, which is the other reason I was shy of approaching Ricky or responding to him because I had been so close to that event.

Poor young David felt the loss of them both as badly as possible, and when last year a young woman persuaded him that her sickly child was his sister he was convinced it must be so, and none of us knew how he was being imposed upon. But it could not work, and the bairn died, and the mother too, and that was over. It hurt him very much, but at the end he was cured of something, and more grown up. So you see he had a great deal to contend with. In the end, if I had a son of my own he would fit very well. Which leads nicely to the next bit.

Ricky and I were by then too busy washing dishes and wondering about each other to notice what was going on in David's mind. But he knew better than either of us what was going on in our minds. I was holding back, you see, because I had attended poor Elizabeth, and it still wasn't right to want to replace her in Ricky's life, even seven years later. Or in David's life, for that matter. And I couldn't believe what I felt and thought I must be misunderstanding myself — and I was.

It was David who settled the matter. He proposed to us both one evening in the surgery, saying he didn't fancy wheeling the pram up the aisle, and what about making an honest man out of his father? When I asked him how he knew I was pregnant, he said his father obviously was, and he went by that.

Now Jeannie, I have the pram, and I have its occupant, and I can tell you that having one your own self is different from helping at the confinement of others. It's called Elizabeth Clare (Lyddy), and young David dotes on it (as I said), and I am jealous, until it becomes putrid and then he takes a scunner to her and gives her back and I am happy to do all the smelly bits, because I dote on it too. They do homework together, and David is teaching her to cry in Algebra and laugh in Latin (he learns it because he will be a doctor, and says Latin is the language of the giblets), and maintains she knows all the Greek letters like puke and dribble. All in all it isn't quite like home as we knew it, but I wouldn't change it, and I can't believe it is all still true. Ricky begins to understand why I wake in the night and burst into tears of acute happiness. I can't believe it's me having all this happen to me.

Of course the father dotes on it too. I am afraid it is spoilt already.

This is the invitation to the christening. David is to be a godfather, Eileen Watson, the wife of the good farmer I mentioned, is one godmother, their adopted son the stotherd (Nellie Jack John, or John Cherry if you don't know him well enough, who is a nice lad with a stranger history than David) is another godfather, and you are the second godmother. We shall arrange matters and times to suit you, except that it's bound to be Church of England, not what we were brought up to be. And you won't blame me if I want you to meet my family and love them as much as I do, which I hope I can do without losing any of my affection for my only sister.

Kirstie (not Mackenzie but Wix)

Of course stay here, I'll put the kids in one room and you can have David's.

P.S. I don't read my wife's correspondence, unless she makes me. I'll explain that I'm so delighted with her that I often wake up in fits of terminal laughter, when I think what I did in marrying her, so it's often quite a comedy – Ricky.

P.S.S. You won't have been able to read that medical scribble, but it's true – K.

TWO

'Not displeasure,' Dr Tate was saying, by Jingle Beck, his anorak billowing in the wind that danced down the gill, his hair lifting at the front like the economical quiff of a cartoon. 'More a sense of despair, Heseltine – and watch what you are doing.'

'Sir,' said Keith, being as steady as possible, carrying the tripod part of the surveying instrument along the edge of the water, through reeds and grass, among rocks and tussocks, water and slime.

'Single file,' Dr Tate shouted back at the class. He walked beside Keith, in double file. He doesn't know he's doing that, thought Keith.

'Pitiable,' said Dr Tate, following on from despair. 'Every year it's the same. Watch your step, Heseltine.'

Keith was on a flat lawn of green grass. Dr Tate had got knee-deep among some miniature ravines, and assumed that everyone should be the same.

Jingle Beck wandered among little rounded hills, the steep sides of the gill opening out as the class went up it. Sheep looked up from eating, or down from grassy knolls, still chewing, then looked away unalarmed, disgusted by the file of scholars.

Among the little hills lay a flatter bay of moorland, with Dr Tate's destination standing in it, the Jingle Stones, thin, short, frequent, and black.

'Not feeling big,' David was saying. 'Still like marks on a map.'

'Big enough,' said Dr Tate, 'not to make so many silly mistakes.'

People were complaining that the stones were getting further away, not closer, as they approached.

'They are four hundred and thirty-nine metres north north west,' said Dr Tate, kneeling on a tussock of grass with his satellite position finder. 'I've checked it out.' All the same, the stones had a receding air to them. Dr Tate tapped the GPS, and held it to his ear.

Someone muttered that certain people needed a GPS to find the toilet. Dr Tate said, 'That's enough of that, person called Metcalfe.'

The person called Metcalfe shook her much-crimped head of hair and said, 'Except the sheep. They poo anywhere.' She trudged through alien grasses, and seemed far out of her element. Dr Tate snorted inaudibly. David sensed his own irritation; then wondered which element the Metcalfe person was out of, school or hillside.

All at once the stones were among the class, looking down, tall, wide, and grey as winter even with the summer sun striking through among them and warming a red underskin. Keith said that the class had not come to the stones, but the stones to the class. Dr Tate, gathering people round him with waving of the arms and finger semaphore, said it was the weather, not folklore, Heseltine. 'But these are the Jingle Stones. Make six separate surveys of them, position, height, dimensions. I shall supervise the instrument. The results will display the usual confusion and lack of accuracy – not an instruction, only a forecast. Remember that some of your terminal results depend on course work, not only on one exam after years of idleness.'

He went round and among the stones for the rest of the morning, telling people to get the tripod upright, it has a spirit level in it, it has another one there, and a third one here, and all three must be right, no it is not impossible, the foot is sinking into the ground? put a block under it. Why are you lying down, you Metcalfe person?

'Noises under the ground, sir,' she told him. 'There are people there, sir.'

'Not people,' said Dr Tate. 'That is theophany, the speech of God.'

'Sir!' said the Metcalfe person, shocked at such a frivolous response. 'It sounded like a toilet.'

'The rational explanation is the sound of underground water,' said Dr Tate. 'Though why we should want rational explanations in school begins to defeat me. And you are old enough not to have to think of toilets every time you hear running water.'

'It's a tune,' said the girl, listening again, like a small child.

Now, said Dr Tate, he would prepare a probability graph, with the help of the GPS, although since its built-in error was more than half the diameter of the circle, the system could not resolve single stones, only approximately the position of the whole circle.

For a time he tried to form an average of the positions of the stones using the GPS. But he had to give up, saying that the batteries were failing intermittently. 'Some person has been playing with it,' he concluded, shaking the instrument in the ritual and superstitious way that often cures machinery. 'It is giving the same reading as at the farmhouse, Swang.'

'Stone circles are like that,' said Keith. 'It stands to reason.'

'Nonsense,' said Dr Tate, putting the device back into his pocket. 'Batteries are known to fail, and it's no more than that. Or a bad attack of anagram.'

He went round the groups, checking manually. 'I think we'll have a better result this year,' he said. 'But the figures are all yours. While you are gathering them, recall the original purpose of any stone circle, which is what? Apart from jumbling its letters to make the word "electronics".'

Nobody knew, except about hating anagrams, but that did not matter. They were told about the simple open-air places of worship of their ancestors, the cathedrals of a former age, the palaces of pagan gods, the solemn gathering places of a cultivated race, the holy observatories and calendar-makers of the golden age; and have you finished? it's time we were getting back.

David saw the bus come up from the town and negotiate the track to Swang Farm, where it turned and waited. Only he and Keith, it seemed, knew where to look in this landscape. Apparently only they and Dr Tate had been to the Jingle

Stones before this day. Most of the group found this region, a mile or two from home, as alien as the Sahara.

'Spider-hunting,' said the person called Metcalfe, dredging something from the back of her mind.

'It was just on the hill up there that I got struck,' said David, calmly, easily, without having to consider it. 'They say.'

'You were killed,' said Dr Tate. 'I had to tell the school about that. And then you came back. I expect I said complimentary things about you, but it's the right thing to do on those occasions, and you mustn't take them to heart, Wix. If you wanted them to remain true you should have stayed dead.'

'I'll remember next time,' said David.

'But good heavens,' Dr Tate was by then saying to someone else, 'you should have drawn to the scale we decided upon. Come on, everyone, you've finished now, bring me the maps. Let's hope, thank you, thank you – no, you can carry the board, give the clips to Wix – let's hope that apart from Metcalfe's extraordinary effusions we have a uniformity of result. Heseltine will lead, single file again.'

Dr Tate knocked at the front door of Swang Farm, which only formal visitors used. 'How do you do, Mrs Watson?' he said to Eileen, when she had wrenched it open, ready to repulse stock-feed salesmen. 'We've drawn our maps, and counted the stones. Possibly.'

'Oh,' said Eileen, 'thank you for the key back.'

'I haven't a key,' said Dr Tate, empty-handed. 'The school office rang to ask if we could come, that's all.'

'It's a way of speaking,' said Eileen. 'You ask for the key, then

13

you give it back. You've to be careful, with boggarts and that about.'

'Metaphorical,' said Dr Tate.

'Did you?' said Eileen. 'The key is for the gate, but we don't know rightly where that gate is, and the stones are a fence to keep something inside.'

'A fence?' said Dr Tate.

'And,' said Eileen, having her say, 'when Frank's grandad took one of them to make a gatepost, something came and lived in here with us. It's quiet now, but it's a boggart when it has a mind to. And you can't count the stones, except on Midsummer Eve, and it's better not to then. If you get it right, you wish you hadn't, the tale goes. But it doesn't matter what lads and lasses do.'

'We shall accept those facts,' said Dr Tate, getting into the bus, 'with thanks again. Even the person called Metcalfe will accept them.'

'It's the biz,' said the person called Metcalfe.

'Now then, Sally,' said Eileen. 'My half-cousin,' she explained to Dr Tate.

'And the school is much obliged for letting us visit,' Dr Tate went on, ignoring information about any Metcalfe. 'We left the stones as we found them, no litter, no graffiti, no souvenirs.'

'They'll shuffle all night,' said Eileen. 'With folk tramping in there.'

'I can understand that,' said Dr Tate, 'I'm the same myself after being all day at school.' He climbed on to the step of the bus. 'I'll be back again with another group in a year or two, Mrs Watson, just after the millennium.'

'I don't know that we'll be here,' said Eileen, shaking her head slowly. 'Our lease will run out by then, and I don't think Frank can renew it. I don't know where we'll go. You'll have to ask the next people for the key.'

'Then I will,' said Dr Tate. He closed the bus door. 'What does she mean?' he asked no one in particular, 'shuffle all night?'

The bus chewed its way along the lane. Dr Tate looked at the maps, staring and comparing.

'Have your dinners, lunches, what-have-you,' he said, when they got to the school and he was rolling the papers up. 'Then come straight back to the class room, and we'll go through this, this rigmarole, this travesty of effort, this jumble of inaccuracy, this misleading bundle of infantile ineptitude. You'd think that what Mrs Watson said had some factual value and reference, since no group has agreed with another about the position of the stones, their relationship, or,' and he unravelled the sheets again and counted, 'even the number.'

'But that's what she said,' said Keith.

'Impoverished head of tiny north country secondary school goes off his head,' said Dr Tate. 'Disarray claims another victim. I am right, says Doctor of Philosophy. Isn't that so, Wix?'

'Eileen is right,' said David. 'If you can't count the stones how do you decide where they are?'

'If both sets of facts are right,' said Keith, 'common sense and tradition, then they must be facts about different things.'

15

'There will be only one set of facts,' said Dr Tate, 'one authentic set of Jingle Stones, and one result in your books. We must all fight off despair, even if it is the specific alternative to quantum physics. But perhaps it's best to have only fragments of certainty, because nothing is as it seems.'

No one knew what he meant.

'I wonder,' said Keith, going off to the dining hall with David, 'what Eileen means about the lease running out. It can't, can it?'

'Your father will know,' said David. 'He's the solicitor who takes Frank's rent money. Frank often talks about it.'

'Next term,' said Keith. 'Fridays, when I begin work in the office. I'll ask then.'

THREE

They all went into the church together, David, Dr Wix, Kirstie and her sister Jeannie, and Keith. David carried the pink plastic hand baggage, casual but proud, swinging his arm about more carefully than he affected. He looked down at what was inside, making a face to please it. It shook its arms in unison. It still had not separated left from right, inside from outside, and it was really sleepy-time in the afternoon.

'My mother brought me here for it when I was this size,' said David.

His own mother had been in this same church garden, these seven or eight years now; and it had been seven or eight years before that that she had brought David to the church. Keith touched David's arm, because no one quite fills another's empty space; and he knew what was written in the little graveyard they had just come through.

'I shan't drop it,' said David, thinking Keith meant that, giving the baby another parabola to prove it. The baby smiled at the bright April sky above.

Dark blue smoke rose smelly against that light blue, a brisk tractor engine thundered, and locked wheels with huge treads grazed the gravel road. The engine stopped and the cab door slopped shut. The dog Jip circled behind the glass and sat on the driving seat.

Nellie Jack John appeared, pulling on a jacket and clawing at his collar and tie. He was more at home in a loose milking kytle, and shop jackets were not tailored to his shoulders.

'I isn't late,' he said, meaning that if he was he certainly did not mean to be.

'You're well in time,' said Kirstie, stepping up and taking him by the neck. 'Who put this on you?' she asked, bandaging the tie round his throat, like setting a fracture, 'stand up,' getting the limb of his neck upright, 'this end should be longer.'

'I did it mesel',' said Nellie Jack John. 'In that much of a rush wi' lambing, and my Mam so thrang wi' that she couldn't get, and Frank, he said it went like a coo-tee.'

Nellie Jack John shook his head and settled his collar with big fingers. 'When I were in t'regiment,' he said, because he had been a soldier long ago, when he was a little younger, 'I were smart.'

'You're a dandy now,' said Kirstie. 'For a stot-herd. I'll stand in for Eileen.' Eileen was Nellie Jack John's adoptive mother, and was to be a godmother.

Martin Malpass stood in the church doorway with his vicar's white church gear on, smoothing a white pleat where his tummy pushed it out a little.

'Is this the young lady?' he asked, beaming very well at the baby. 'She's charming. Find a pew while I take Keith to the vestry and tell him what to do.'

Keith was not expecting to be separated and trained, even in the place of worship he did not attend, but Martin Malpass took him beyond some arches, and a moment later was saying, 'No, no, you don't have to dress up, Keith. You'll know when to come in, and what you'll be doing.'

Keith was muttering about method being one thing, and ceremony another. Three matches were struck, two of them damp, the third fizzling into life. Their strange incense floated about the aged church air.

Nellie Jack John looked into the carrycot and pulled the cover back from the baby's face with his thick careful fingers. 'Tha's fatting up,' he said, used to lambs. 'Isn't tha?'

Martin Malpass came out from the vestry alone. He stood by the stone bowl of the font. 'The young person,' he reminded them, waiting to carry out the purpose of the visit.

'I'll present it,' said David.

'A shame to wake her,' said Kirstie, because the baby had closed both eyes.

'We all have to wake up,' said Martin Malpass, in a clerical remark, full of meaning and parable. 'And I have a service in Gunthwait at five. We measure time in hours, but seconds are measured in grace.'

David felt a shiver walk across him. It was partly the cold church air, and partly because so much was gathered together, father, new mother, his own mother being not far away outside and pleased, and the baby stapling them firmly together, past, present, and future.

The woken baby smiled at him to show it understood, but

would forgive him for now. Just to go on with, she hiccuped, burped, and foamed at the mouth.

'Och,' said Kirstie, wiping away bubbles, and dabbing at David's jacket.

I shall remember this, David was thinking. I am happy. It is right. I am calm and contented. I have all three parents, and my friends, my sister has been sick on my sleeve, and this is now and for ever.

A shower cloud flew across the sun. The church filled with shadows rich and gloomy. Prayer books and hymnals breathed out their compost of damp years. Spring rain rattled the faded gleams of the windows.

'Elizabeth Clare,' David said. 'Lyddy for short.'

'The godparents?' said Martin Malpass. 'Two godmothers, one godfather, are customary.'

'Mam couldn't get,' said Nellie Jack John. 'Eileen. On wi' lambing and that.'

'I'll be a proxy for her,' said Kirstie.

'And the other?' said Martin Malpass, looking enquiringly at the only other candidate, Jeannie.

There was a double shriek from outside. Martin Malpass wondered what it was. Godmothers? his eyebrows asked. Triplets?

'I've two pet lambs in t'tractor box for t'lile lass,' said Nellie Jack John. 'They've gitten their bottle of milk but want back wi' their mams.'

'Well, bless them too,' said Martin Malpass, in a professional way. 'Is this the other godmother?'

'My sister Jeannie,' said Kirstie.

The godfather was Nellie Jack John, called John Cherry for the occasion. 'I've had a go before,' he said. 'But there wasn't time to do owt mich.' His first godchild had not lived long after the ceremony, and that ceremony had been because she was not to last long.

'We'll get on, then,' said Martin Malpass.

A moment later David was standing next to him, holding the baby, and looking into the bowl of the font, on its egg-cup leg of stone.

In the bottom of the lead lining lay a circle of shining water, still as ice. That was what David expected, but there was more. A magic picture in it held his eye, a brightness like sky, a looking-glass glimmer beyond reality, strung with cracks like cobweb, in and out of focus.

'David,' said Martin Malpass. David was staring and not handing the baby over.

Kirstie was assuming that the baby had become putrid at this inconvenient moment, and David wanted to hand her back for attention.

It was not that. The baby remained perfect.

A fuzzy ache stood between David's eyes. Light on the water and in it confused him, forming in the apparent depth a glow that created more light. He shook his head, to break the magic picture apart.

He lifted his eyes and the curve of the church roof, the arches of the aisle, heaped over him, like the vault of a cave. He knew he had been here before, knew what happened next, without being certain which was real – being here, or in another place or time. He had become a magic picture himself, lifting from the flat page of actuality into a three-dimensional image with space and depth and duration.

'Just a feeling,' he was about to say, because if you know what it is you know what is actual. The persuasion that he was in another place and time began to recede. He steadied his mind. He refused the illusion, the memory of the cave, the time he had been there, the reason for it. He flattened his picture of himself. 'Nothing.' Later on, he decided, I'll think about it later on.

He began to hand Lyddy to Martin Malpass, all the passage of impressions over in less than a second's hesitation.

Before he had hoisted the baby more than a very little way Keith began coming from the vestry, carefully carrying a burning candle, wanting the flame to stand stiffly carved in light, as a flame should be, ideal, unflickering.

I have wanted that before, Keith was thinking. When was it? Was it only now? Has this happened before as well as now?

Keith looked towards David, and for both of them a different place and time became the reality. Another event was gathering in the filament of flame.

David was no longer in church. That vault was becoming the cave under the hills, with Keith coming for him across a rough floor, shuffling rubble underfoot. David saw both church and cave, two competing realities, and had to change his mind again about what he would deal with first.

He had to finish what he was in the cave for, a simple action that would restore . . . he did not know what . . . but it was in the circle of water; he could see it by candlelight, and almost understand something more like taste than meaning.

'David,' said Keith, almost in the cave too, having to choose one place or another, but hanging between them, not knowing which was more real, more here, and most now.

David was between the baby and the urgent need to deal with what was in the pool of radiant water. Somehow, perhaps, he could do both. He reached out his hands to lift what he must get, his hands reaching for it, to hold it, to deliver . . .

Martin Malpass was reaching towards him. Nellie Jack John had an arm against him. The baby called out, far and far away. Lambs cried outside. Sunlight ripped the church windows open and burnt out the sky.

David was beyond the church, beyond the cave, on the hillside above the Jingle Stones, some years ago.

FOUR

Broad daylight and open air, and David was looking into the radiance coming out of the hill, at what was in it, flying towards him. He wanted Keith to see it too, and appreciate the wonderful presence.

'Listen,' he said, because it was sound as much as sight. 'Listen, that's it.'

Keith was taking no notice, standing stock still, like one of the Jingle Stones a little further along the hill, part of the spiky skyline.

'This is it,' said David, explaining, pointing with both hands, both arms, at what had discovered him, the sparkled beauty of it before his eyes, the crashing but subtle music of excitement.

Keith, or a Jingle Stone, looked dumbly back at him, not sensible enough to be clearly seen; Keith at his most obtuse.

David was seeing what he had been seeking without knowing for weeks now. He had been gazing at it in a candle flame, drawing closer to it, but not finding the burning palace, the lights of another world, or meeting the inhabitant coming towards him. That world had reached him now. I was born for it, David was thinking. It chose me without knowing I could help. But whether this was now memory or now happening he could not tell.

Keith might help better, being so matter-of-fact; but he was standing aside, not sharing what was being revealed to David inside the hill.

It was all David had ever wanted, and he said so, in as many words. He was unable to describe what it was, what the light was, what the sounds were. He did not know the language or the colours, and could identify no substance. He knew that it was burning him, flowing through his body and mind, as if he had entered the flame of the candle.

Keith stood, and merely looked wretched, while David was arriving somewhere he had never imagined, yet a place where he had always wanted to be.

'Keith,' he said, 'look at the butterfly, look.' Broad jewelled wings rose and fell before his eyes, transparent and bright. They came out of the hill and stood above him. He stretched his hands up, to be part of this splendid reality.

'This is home,' he said. But he knew Keith had probably gone away to do something sensible and dull, good and necessary but without light or purpose.

'This is everywhere,' David said. But this time he detected uncertainty in his speech. In fact it was not speech, but a thought. 'Everywhere and everything that I could want.' But he was trying to be changed even further in the twinkling of an eye, be surrounded by a lustre of joy, hear wonders beyond the charm of music, and be welcomed to a broader home than his own, surely better than the world.

But his own self warily stood back, not joining in. If only I hadn't brought me along, he supposed. Perhaps that bit isn't me, but Keith being sensible and unselfish as usual, doing something for me, not for himself.

The butterfly above his head moved with menacing slow grace, its bright patterns warning of danger.

'Keith,' he said, trying to say what it was, that he saw it, that it touched him with a frail invisible thread.

Light went away. Round him things moved and changed in darkness. He was snared and wrapped with a palpable flaccid web; he felt its nervous reaction to him, almost felt its pain when it touched him like a communication, with a message

He almost heard the message, almost understood why he was obeying it. He saw his hands gathering pieces from a pool of water at his feet, a pool of light, without understanding what they were doing, or knowing what they were gathering. He had the pieces in his hand, ready to put together, ready to understand what they made, why they made it, its purpose. He heard them grate together gently, he saw them shine with fragile translucency. Then he was interrupted.

Keith was coming towards him, carrying a candle, Keith picking his way across the floor of a cave, Keith with darkness flooding after him. Keith in the church . . . but there was something important to do before going back there; something in David's hands, to assemble, to release, to restore . . .

What was in David's hands tinkled and splashed back into the water, and the frail lambency faded.

Moving shadows turned into pillars of glittering rock, from

roof to floor. A flash of light struck Keith and he fell down at the edge of a rock table.

He was up again at once, his eyes wet in the candlelight, his fingers red where he held his wound, a candle tipping in the hand of that arm. David smelt blood.

David let go what he held. Stone fell to the floor of the cave, into the water, across the rock table. Something retreated from his mind, drawn from his skull with mental and physical pain; clamour, guilt, sorrow, blame, and all at once the new silence of the cave, burst on him like a shout.

'Oh,' said David, wanting to show Keith that nothing strange had happened, that nothing had perturbed him, not admitting pain, uttering foolish babbling words himself, waking from dream. 'You've come, have you? I thought you wouldn't be long. I came about a minute ago. Did you see how you were got here, because I didn't notice much?'

He could no longer move his hands. Delay had settled in the bones of his palm, the sluggish weight of the whole world filled his fingers, like time itself settling there. What he had held in the cave he no longer had in the church.

Keith was in the church with him, with a candle, and someone was holding David's shoulders. Everything had gone wrong here too, and come apart. Keith had walked in here too, drawing things together, pulling them apart. David had nothing in his hands, and his head was empty too.

He was made to sit in a pew, and his hollow head put between his knees, as if he had fainted. What did I drop, he wondered, in this cold building, or that lost cave?

He had dropped his sister. She was cheerful about it, her nappy full of holy water from the font, and Kirstie changing it.

'What did she say?' asked David, trying to be sensible yet sparky in the wan reality of life.

'Nothing,' said Keith, standing there complete and steady, no blood on his arm, no tears to his eyes, the stocky candle flickering and smoking on the prayer book shelf of the pew.

'Shall we carry on?' said Dr Wix.

'We don't usually do total immersion,' said Martin Malpass, looking at the graceful seconds pulsing through his watch.

David sipped a silver cup of water. 'I'll stay here, and you hold Trouble,' he said, raising his head, cold running up his back, then warmth, giving the baby to his father.

Lyddy sang a little hymn, protested at having her face made wet, and Keith blew out the candle, its work done.

FIVE

John Cherry was in the house, godfathering lambs beside the kitchen fire. Kirstie and Jeannie were upstairs making a bed for Jeannie. 'I've put you in the nursery with the baby,' Kirstie told David.

'She talks in her sleep,' said David, bringing in coal for the fires.

In the kitchen, they were beginning tea.

'Jeannie says I've lost my Scottishness,' said Kirstie. 'Because there are no girdle scones.'

'We were off to fight the Scotch, once over, or mebbe t'French,' said Nellie Jack John, not listening very well, busy by the fire.

'Just for now wash your hands,' said Kirstie. 'Where's my baby?'

Baby and lambs were in the box by the fire, milky and asleep. 'Right enough,' said Nellie Jack John, stroking all three.

'It's time for gifts,' Jeannie said. She had brought a silver spoon with a Scottish hallmark.

Nellie Jack John had a lump of pinkish crystal in his pocket. It was like a diamond, if diamonds were shaped like the things on playing cards, solid but nearly transparent, pointed top and bottom, with four edges at the middle. He laid it on the table.

'Jonty found it in the lead mines,' he said, 'and gave it to me for luck. It were t'best he ever saw.'

Light from the lamp shone through it, drawing a hesitant shadow on the cloth, not quite in focus.

David stared at the shadow, trying to pull its refraction straight. 'I'm reminded of something, I don't know what,' he said. 'So I can't be reminded of anything, but I am.'

'It's an octahedron,' said Keith. 'A primary school shape.' But no one wanted to think it was solid.

'Them's from my Mam,' said Nellie Jack John. He meant the lambs, awkwardly asleep in the box, with tight curls and jointy legs with fingerless feet that hung numb from the last angle of the limb. They still had their tails.

They were for Lyddy to buy and sell to put money by, Nellie Jack John said, for her own farm when she needed a flock. They would live at Swang Farm until they were sold, and the profits put aside to buy other lambs to rear.

'She'll get an orf,' said Dr Wix. 'You catch them from lambs. But she'll have it by now, so leave her where she is.'

'She's to get it over with,' said Nellie Jack John. For him it was settled that she would be a shepherdess. 'She'll need a lile dog next. My sisters had pet lambs. They put the brass by, for when they were married, if they lived that long.'

'Sisters, John?' said Kirstie. 'I didn't know you had any.'

'Do you mean they didn't live?' Jeannie asked, carefully, but sure he had said that.

'Not all,' said Nellie Jack John. 'Yah time I got back tiv Eskeleth of a Friday night from t'coalpits at Tan Hill and they were leading away a cart from our house, wi' my three lile sisters in't, all smittled wi't'measle. I last saw them the Sunday night before. When I left they were still asleep and alive, and then gone by I got home.'

No one had anything to say to that. Keith wondered how they worked out about the sheep money. David was deciding he still knew nothing about Nellie Jack John, or what had happened to him.

'Not long ago,' said Kirstie. 'For you.'

'About four or five year, my time,' said Nellie Jack John. 'Hundreds by yours.'

'How many were left when you were last home?' Jeannie asked.

'Two wyes and a bull,' said Nellie Jack John. Two lasses and a lad. 'Yan like that,' pointing to Lyddy, 'and a canny lile lad that hadn't grown his hair yet, bald as a drum. I stopped home a bit wi'em, and then I went for a soldier.'

He had joined the army to help send Scotchmen out of the country again, and lived in Garebrough castle with the regiment.

'Us lads thought there was the king's treasure under t'castle. They'd felted King Arthur away there a right lot of years before, and no one found him or his brass. I went underground wi't'drum, and walked on in t'dark. I found a candle burning, but no treasure, and no king. When I came out at yon end I met these two lads, laiting of summat.'

31

Looking for something, Keith told Jeannie.

'I was sadly out of my time,' said Nellie Jack John, rocking his head. 'Right out of reckoning.'

'We didn't know what we were looking for,' said David. 'There was a noise in the field, and the ground swelling up. We thought it might be a fountain coming.'

'It were mesel,' said Nellie Jack John. 'We had a fight about nowt. Next day these two brought my breacus.'

'Breakfast,' David told Jeannie.

'Aye, that,' said Nellie Jack John. 'The worst thing you could ha' done.'

'You were wet and hungry,' said Keith, 'so we did. Was it wrong? You ate it. You never said.'

'I'd ha' framed better without it,' said Nellie Jack John. 'If I hadn't been gant and eaten thy bacon and supped thy tea I might ha' walked home clear. But if thou takes owt to eat or sup yon side, then thou'l't not git back; and I had thy breacus, and I's here yet. I'll not get back tiv Eskeleth in my proper time.'

'Other things had happened,' said Dr Wix. 'When John came out, he had changed time, and he changed time for other things too.'

'He brought a candle out with him,' said David.

Something flickered like a flame deep in his mind, a light glinting, indicating but not revealing a hidden source. 'Like Keith this afternoon.' But that was not quite what had moved in his mind. The light, the pulses of information from somewhere else, what he had failed to complete in that cave two or three years since, were all related through that candle. He had no idea how to sort matters out. Only, far off in his mind, was the certainty that he should – if he could remember how – if his mind could tell him what it knew.

Dr Wix began to talk of disturbances in the district about that time, of stolen pigs, wild boar in the town market, giants being seen. 'They must all be connected, and come out of the past.'

'Or the recent future,' said Keith. 'If time runs backwards it must run forward too.'

'Or things from the past wouldn't be going to come up in front of us,' said David. 'The past of the future can still be in the future.'

'David was struck by lightning, above Swang, near the Jingle Stones,' said Dr Wix, after no one had worked out what David meant, except that it was true. 'Keith saw it, Frank Watson saw it, a hiker saw it.'

'David just went,' said Keith. 'He shouted, and I saw a crack in the sky, not lightning. Frank Watson carried me down to Swang, and I was sick all night. Everybody thought lightning, but it was a black mark, a crack in the sky.'

'There was an inquest,' said Dr Wix. 'It proved he was dead, and struck by lightning.' His face crumpled at the recollection, as it had stayed for months after the event. Then he grinned and went on, 'But for some reason he made a very inefficient job of it, and here he is. Keith got him back.'

'Never got my lile sisters back,' said Nellie Jack John. 'But they go on tumbling in my mind.'

'I went back with a candle,' said Keith, after a moment, and when Nellie Jack John nodded to him. 'The candle Nellie Jack John brought out with him.'

'It was just a candle at first,' said David. 'But when I looked into it, it was looking into me as well.'

Keith had looked in the candle too, after David had gone, and it had called him in turn, months later, through the night into the hillside, to find David in a cave. Shuddering into their burial places had been a ghostly rout of armed and armoured figures, the court of Nellie Jack John's ancient king, in its tomb under the hill.

Keith had been cut with a sword as he settled the candle into its socket and laid sleep on the king and his squadron of knights.

Candle, socket, water, font, David remembered, following Keith's thoughts, his own jumbled in his mind.

Nellie Jack John had been in the same cave, on a marathon into unreachable time past, the home he could never find. They had turned him in his flowing track, and brought him out again, like steering a comet out of its fiery groove, bringing it to rest on the ground. Or to Swang Farm, to be more clear, where he had entered the family and been adopted.

'Keith coming with a church candle,' said David, 'the church was like a cave, being found by Keith, just as I was going to do something wonderful.'

'He's never done anything wonderful yet,' said Keith. 'So he must have been going to do it then.'

'With any luck,' said Dr Wix, 'he won't do it now, so we're saved from it.'

'That was all,' said David. Stone roof, candle, light in pools of water, turned just below the threshold of understanding. 'Just a sudden memory, a butterfly, those metallic diffraction colours, but just in black and white. I can't think of it.'

'Don't,' said Kirstie. 'Havers, Davy.'

'Havers,' said David. 'Where's my skin and blister?'

Lyddy woke when Nellie Jack John lifted her lambs away. 'One last smoothe,' he said, 'and they'll be ready to eat by winter.'

Her little hands stroked farewell to them. Nellie Jack John took the lambs to the tractor, and banged it into life.

Kirstie took Lyddy to bath her and search for sheep diseases.

SIX

Eileen Watson had the uniform spread on the kitchen table at Swang, where Nellie Jack John had dumped it, and was shaking her head over it.

'It should get washed,' she said, for the third time. 'What if folk see it.'

'That's what it's for,' said Nellie Jack John, putting his modern leg alongside the ancient breeches. 'By, I was a lile fellow in them days.'

'You were a big lad then, and you're just a very big lad now,' said Frank Watson. 'Now, mother, it doesn't matter about getting washed. You'd spoil the set of the cloth, or summat.'

'Cool wash,' said Eileen. 'It can't come to harm as wool. There's never owt gone from here that wasn't clean through, lamb or egg or rag.'

Nellie Jack John and David were rolling up the tunic, with Eileen trying to help and hinder, and Keith acting as peacekeeper. He was used to his mother, he said, who used housework as a lifestyle.

'That seam wants a thread across it,' Eileen was saying, trying to get the uniform under her control.

'It'll gan to the museum split and dirty,' said Nellie Jack John. 'A soldier's uniform gets foul. Just a pity there isn't a great hoil where I got a wound from a Scotch spear or owt. But I niver got to a battle. I'd ha'showed them.'

'Such a state,' said Eileen. 'They'll blame me.'

'Now then, mother,' said Nellie Jack John, 'thou was niver any good wi' a Scotch spear. You'd best brew a pot of tea, to give us summat to go on.'

The uniform, nearly two hundred and fifty years old, was going to the regimental museum in town. The boots were going too, and the regimental drum and drumsticks.

Eileen scratched at a mark on the cloth with a fingernail. Nellie Jack John took her hand away and sent her to put the kettle on the fire. 'Don't be so fond,' he said. 'We'd to live and sleep in yon.'

'That's why they should be washed,' said Eileen.

Eileen spread a cloth and put cake on the table. She glanced into the shadow corners, expecting soldiers with blacked faces to lurch from the darkness and take her kitchen over. The uniform was rolled up into vivid supermarket bags.

Major Chapman was not dressed in uniform. He was also far smaller than Nellie Jack John. 'I thought we wouldn't make it too official,' he said, to explain his lack of uniform. He looked at the supermarket plastic bags, but he said nothing. You can't get more unofficial than Safeway. Keith looked round, because this was the museum church of his father's army, and his grandfather's.

Nellie Jack John looked about him, remembering the building.

'By God, aye,' he said, fingering a pillar where a pew still remained. 'I remember I'd my head rattled on here once ower. I'd lit up a pipe from a candle, and I got sike a twilt off our sergeant there's blood on the wood yet.' He looked down at Major Chapman again, remarked that he'd been but a lad then, to remind everyone that he wouldn't stand for it now.

'Yes,' said Major Chapman.

'Now then,' said Nellie Jack John, to show that he had got here, understood who Major Chapman was, and was going to remain unofficial. 'T'stuff is in t'bags, sithee. It's a bit ramm, but I wouldn't let her wesh it.'

Major Chapman was pleased. 'We'll sort all that out,' he said. 'We can clean and restore. It's not often we get uniforms so fresh.'

Nellie Jack John pulled a bag off the top of the drum. 'I'll not sound it,' he said. 'T'skin is cracking and if I bray it that'll finish it. I can get a better skin, sithee.'

'Our people know about that,' said Major Chapman.

'Aye?' said Nellie Jack John, not believing him.

'It's the same army,' said Major Chapman, 'it's been going on here without a break ever since your time, Mr Cherry.'

'Well,' said Nellie Jack John, 'don't tell it where you got the gear. I left without getting killed, and I'd get whipped or shot. But I'll get you a better skin for t'drum-head.'

Major Chapman was last seen putting the bags in his car, bravely pretending they were not his shopping and did not smell.

38

It was Saturday afternoon, and the person called Metcalfe prodded the till and chatted to customers at the chemist's checkout. David was buying a film, and Keith had volunteered to find a packet of nappies to save time, because Nellie Jack John was outside on the tractor to give them a ride home, mounted high, his face looking aloofly down the market place, his eyes now and then flickering to the chemist's doors or windows.

'Blooming hopeless,' Sally Metcalfe said, shaking her head when Keith added his purchase to the film. She shouted down the shop, 'Molly, gerra packet er them girls' clouts, eh,' and came back to Keith to explain that David's sister was a girl, you gorra read the packet, eh.

'I just took their word for it,' said Keith, conscious that the whole shop was looking at him.

'You made a joke,' said David.

Sally had nothing to do for a moment. She looked out of the window. 'In't he a hunk?' she said, gazing at someone outside, high on the tractor. 'Tell 'im, eh?'

The packet, clearly marked 'GIRL', and with a wide border of limp pink, came to her hand, and she ran it through the bar-code reader.

'He's waiting of you,' she said, taking money. 'What are you off to do? One of them spider hunts up at them stones, eh?'

'Spider hunts?' said David.

'My grandma was saying,' said Sally. 'In them days. Big spiders.' Then she was on to the next customer's soap, 'It's a lovely smell, but it does cost, eh?' half-admiration, half-envy.

Nellie Jack John gave them a ride to David's house at the top of the town.

'Spider hunting,' said Keith, when the tractor engine stopped clattering and they got out of the box. 'I've heard of that, in the back of my mind.'

'That's where the spiders are,' said David.

'There's a vast of them on the tops,' said Nellie Jack John. 'Attercops. They got my uncle Alec when he was a lad, before my time. Attercop hunting is what he went off to do, and never came back. My grandad's lile brother.'

'Where?' David asked.

'Jingle Stones way,' said Nellie Jack John. 'Owt can happen there.'

'Killed by spiders?' said Keith.

'Bottom of a pot hole, more like,' said Nellie Jack John. 'Getting dowks' eggs on the scars, owt. They made stuff up in those days, they hadn't newspapers to tell 'em tales.'

'It'll be some rare species the kids were told to look for,' said Keith. 'Natural history of spiders. It would be just like Dr Tate, if he was alive then.'

'There's always one of them,' said David.

'Know-all people,' said Keith. 'Books on extinct spiders and obscure moths.'

'Obscure maths,' said David. 'Myths.'

Nellie Jack John inspected the baby, accepted a cup of tea, and went on to Swang for the evening milking. 'I'll be up at the Jingle Stones after my dinner tomorrow,' he said. 'Putting up a lamb fence, daft divils. Frank doesn't want to bother with the job, but it's best with a bit of help.'

David settled down with Keith and the baby, to discuss with both of them how to find a formula to draw an ellipse if you knew only the two diameters.

'She won't tell us,' said Keith, after sitting Lyddy up and explaining the matter to her.

'What an ignorant kid,' said David.

'Find the two centres,' said Keith. 'Come on.'

'Just read the packet,' said David. 'See whether it says Boy, Girl, or Genius.'

Keith got to the Jingle Stones by himself. David was baby-sitting and the baby asleep. Nellie Jack John came up after him, with the tractor box full of wood; though not enough, Keith thought, to make any useful enclosure.

'There's plenty,' said Nellie Jack John, without explaining what he intended to do. It was almost as if he didn't know, Keith thought. He knows but doesn't want to explain.

He went on to consider that he would never be a hunk like Nellie Jack John in anyone's eyes, only a solicitor and a solicitor's son, a sort of office person; and was looking at the occasional green shoot of early spring deep in the brown grass, and wondering about spiders, rattling a pocketful of small plastic pill bottles ready to put them in, from his mother's homeopathic store.

But would like to be a hunk, he thought.

Nellie Jack John left the tractor and its wood outside the circle, then came inside.

'You have to find it from inside,' he said, without explaining what it was, as if he were sharing something known to them both. 'But put the fence outside.' He was pacing about, with a pointed stick in his hand. 'Getting the road,' he said. 'Start in t'middle, when I find it. I'll try that first.' He indicated one of the gaps between stones with a nod of the head. He stuck the stick into the ground.

He found the centre by some experiment Keith could not fathom, walking out from it to the stones, and coming back to find another starting place, time and again until he was satisfied.

'Either it's the answer to our ellipse question,' said Keith, 'or you could just have marked it the first time. If you've done it before.'

'You don't want folk finding it,' said Nellie Jack John. When he had found it he would take the stick away, he said. He walked carefully from that place to a gap between stones, and stood in it, looking beyond.

'That's it,' he said. 'Go out round the circle to that gap, then look through at me.'

Nellie Jack John was not one to try silly tricks on people. Keith took him seriously and did as he asked, looking into the circle between two stones.

Nellie Jack John, not very attentively, stepping to the centre he had marked, and began to walk towards Keith.

He vanished. It happened both gradually and immediately. He neither faded nor blinked out, nor went through any stage between. He merely seemed not to exist any more. Then he was visible again, turned round, stepping to the centre, and from it speaking to Keith. 'Where's thou been?' he asked. 'Come through.'

Keith walked through, and down to Nellie Jack John, checking himself for visibility as he went. 'What was it?' he asked.

Nellie Jack John could hardly explain. 'It's yonder,' he said, 'or summat.' He led Keith out from the centre, the way he had gone when he vanished, and on between the stones, where Keith had been standing.

Nothing happened, as far as Keith could tell. They went between the stones, and stepped on the same wiry grass, the same tufts of heather, the identical horizons and a darkening sky.

'Well,' said Keith, thinking he had after all been fooled for no reason, 'what's what?'

Nellie Jack John looked round him 'The tractor,' he said, 'isn't there. We're out at the same spot, but I don't know when it is. It might be yesterday, it might be my own time.'

'It might be tomorrow,' said Keith, keeping his feet still, bending his body to peer round stones, finding no tractor, letting the surface of his mind play with the idea. Nothing deeper wanted to know.

'We just want our lambs back,' said Nellie Jack John, 'if they stray through. So there's a fence to put across the way through to a different spot, that's all. We build it yon side of time. Don't tell my mother, that's all. Just me and Frank fence up each year, and he doesn't stir out so much now. We've got this bother of keeping the farm, and I-don't-know-what about the lease and the rent and that.'

'And the spiders?' said Keith, rattling the brown plastic bottles. 'What about them?'

'If we see them we'll turn back,' said Nellie Jack John, shaking his head sadly at the sight of the little bottles, still knowing things he was not saying. 'We'll get to the middle again and fetch the wood off the tractor, and put the fences up.'

The fence covered three gaps between stones, over in the other era of time. If you came from the centre, Nellie Jack John said, you could go through anywhere along there. 'The place shifts each year,' he said. 'Lambs will turn back at the fence.'

'Present or future?' Keith asked.

'Lambing time,' said Nellie Jack John.

When they came back into the ring of present time, no part of the fence could be seen; nothing showed from the present.

'Impossible,' said Keith, going for another look, when he had confirmed that the tractor was still visible, and he had felt it with his hand, radiator still warm, part of current actuality.

'Take out the stick that marks the middle, when tha comes back,' said Nellie Jack John, dropping a hammer and bag of nails into the tractor box. 'Be right careful. I'm off now and thou can ride down in the tractor box if thou's coming.'

Keith did not hear him. Keith was among the stones, finding the centre of the circle, walking out of it towards the fences, not looking round.

Get a hunk mind, he was thinking. Take yourself in hand, do something by yourself. Not interested in Sally Metcalfe, but one day there'll be somebody.

At the moment there was nobody. The fence was ahead, lamb-high only. A hunky leg over, a graceful sweep with the other, and Keith was beyond it, and walking a hundred paces away on the moor.

Little bottles rattled in his pocket. 'Just get one,' Keith said aloud. 'Extinct.' He knelt in the grass. It was tall, tall to his shoulders, open and wet towards its brown roots, with sucking noises from it. A little beck tinkled teaspoons close by. There was no convenient spider to be made captive.

Keith stood up. As he did so he heard something drop, and without ever seeing it, knew it had gone out of sight.

'Actually time, not sight,' Keith said, quietly to himself, because having the right thoughts might make you lucky; hunky.

The flopping sound, of something dropping out of sight, had been between him and the fence.

Over to the left something else slapped dryly, and the grass moved.

'John,' said Keith, facing that noise. 'Nellie Jack John.'

Behind him, again, another thing made a rustling leathery noise. Keith's throat did the same thing, swallowing nothing. A spasm shook his back, his knees felt empty, and hair moved on his head all by itself, touching his ears.

There was a message, a jittery tapping code, from one site of noise to another, and were responses from further away.

A bare brown back showed fifty feet away. Some low creature was moving towards him. Behind him another showed itself for a moment.

One between him and the fence showed itself too, the round back, the stalky legs of . . .

'Spider hunting,' said Keith; but there was no air in his chest, and no sound came out. The thought was clear, however: enormous spiders were herding him away from the fence.

Keith began to move. His senses were returning, and he did not go the way they wanted. In a desperate and uncalculated way, he ran towards one of them, and it retreated. But as it went, others hurried forward, to surround him. One spoke in a breathy rattle and moved him to one side. But he jumped towards it, and it removed itself.

'They don't know about the fence,' he realised. 'They are making a circle round me. An ellipse.'

Between the spiders, like an invisible web, ran an electric buzzing that made the hair of Keith's arms stand up, that shifted his scalp so that he heard his hair move like bristles.

He backed away from this weapon. He got to the fence side of the hunters, and ran. This was a time for force not athletic grace. He hurled himself along, with the clicking noise following of hollow legs, the rattling of external bones. His own knees brushed past each other, grass tore at his hands when he stumbled and fell.

A claw touched his back. But by then he was at the fence, in the air, spilling brown plastic bottles, and heard himself shriek.

The enemy was on him, fighting hard, biting at his neck, growling, dribbling poison, smelling . . . smelling like a dog.

'Give over, you daft beggar,' Nellie Jack John was saying, pummelling his dog Jip to quieten him, pulling him away.

'Jumping out on folk.'

Keith was sitting up, rubbing his neck. Jip was jumping round him, wanting to continue the romp, shouting with doggy joy.

'He means nowt,' said Nellie Jack John. 'Wants hezzeling.' In his day dogs were trained by beating with hazel wands.

'I know,' said Keith, speaking as breath went in and galloped out of him, 'I thought it was . . .' But he could not say what he thought, because it was too ridiculous. 'I was dreaming.'

Something stronger than dream was with him, something lurking and moving beyond the stones. Something that might stride over fences. He stood on all fours, leapt across the stone circle, and jumped straight into the tractor box. Nellie Jack John climbed into the seat and drove down the hill, into the yard at Swang, Keith cowering behind the safe metal, Jip licking his face and biting his elbows.

'I think I'll go home now,' said Keith, when the engine stopped. 'I never came.' He got on his bike at once and rode away.

'Right,' said Nellie Jack John. 'I niver saw thee.'

A broken hunk went to his own house and ate a large tea, while its mother wondered why it looked so pale. 'You want building up,' she said.

I shall always be drop-dead ugly, the broken hunk decided.

In the morning its mother said, 'Your light was on all night. Turn it off before going to sleep.'

'I will,' said Keith; but some nights it is better not to have darkness near you.

SEVEN

A scabby parchment leaf floated against the window and tapped to come in. Behind it was the autumn darkness of Keith's garden, but the room light showed it leaning on the glass, its dry points scratching like a voice.

David had heard the voice before, and it brought him out of the school work he was buried in.

Keith looked up too. 'What do you mean?' he said.

'Nothing,' said David, carefully. Keith had been nervous of small noises all summer, hearing them above others. 'A leaf talking at the window.'

'Well, shut up,' said Keith, looking, listening, then going back to work. 'You'll wake the thing on the floor.'

The thing on the floor was digging a hole in his mother's old rug, and was awake but happy.

David knew the rattling word accidentally spoken by the leaf. It had said it and stopped its gossip. He went back to the War of the Spanish Succession, but the brittle sound still croaked in his ears, and thoughts that had been still for a long time tumbled again. He laid down his pen and stared at the leaf. Keith should draw his curtains, he thought. Wasting light over the town.

'Look,' said Keith.

'Be quiet,' said David, still wondering about the creaky word, not knowing where to look. 'I'm thinking in black and white, nothing emotional. And I'm looking.'

'You're not,' said Keith. 'While you gawped out of the window, Lyddy stood up by herself, on her hind legs.'

David gave up communicating with the leaf. It had no more to say. The baby now had her knees and her head on the rug, a state that only counted as standing up in some other dimension.

'Just wind,' said David. 'Pat her on the back.'

'She'd puke on me,' said Keith. 'It was a world record, well over four seconds, until gravity took over and she lost it.'

Lyddy fell sideways, wriggled about and said things happily, no more intelligible than a leaf, but less disturbing.

Keith's pen scratched the paper. David could almost hear its words. The leaf at the window sent a chirruping message, a scratch without words.

Keith looked up, aware of the noise.

'It doesn't mean anything,' said David, putting down his pen.

'It's instinct,' said Keith. 'Getting up on your hind legs.'

'That leaf in the window,' said David.

'Leaf doesn't have the instinct of meaning,' said Keith. 'Wind, like you said, yes, standing up, maybe, but instinct, no.'

'If it did have the instinct,' said David, 'it would have purpose behind it.'

'Perhaps it's lost, David, pathetic, O.K.?' said Keith, sharply patient. 'I want to finish this essay. Let it go and find its friends and be happy with them. There's thousands on each tree.'

Lyddy tried to stand up again, but had lost the knack. She yelled and became red in the face. David got down on the floor to tease her with toys.

'Listen Lyddy,' he said, 'Kirstie won't be long. She's gone to Crackpot Hall to make you a ghostly cot and creepy bedroom and find things to screech in the night.'

'You're making her worse,' Keith grumbled.

'It's better than being miserable,' said David. 'Lyddy, there'll be bats in your potty, toads in the wardrobe, goblins running under the floors, and you'll always be accompanied by a skeleton.'

Lyddy joined in a game of Teddy Bear tennis and her skeleton felt better. Keith dropped the bear. Lyddy thought that was perfect, slumped against the coal scuttle and closed her eyes.

The leaf tapped on the glass, and made a questioning squeal.

'It's a message,' said David, because the strange insistence woke thoughts that wanted meaning, that wanted to feel the thread of message touching his face, his wrists.

Keith spoke quietly, not wanting to notice the subject. 'We've dealt with that, and the baby's asleep. Shall we get on with our work?'

'You think it was still only a leaf,' said David. 'You remember the christening.' He was not changing the subject.

'Unforgettable,' said Keith, glad to talk about events he understood. 'You dropped the baby in the font and we treated you for wobblies. Apart from that, I know what you mean. I thought I was going through the cave again, the church being so low and dark, and me doing the candle bit again. It was just a thought, from the past, nothing real.'

'Like the cave,' said David. 'You bringing the candle in again. I dropped something in the cave.'

'And dropped Lyddy in the church to prove it,' said Keith.

'Something wants me to go back and pick it up again and do it right,' said David.

The baby flopped over. David sat her on his knee. She stayed asleep. Keith put coal on the fire and put that to sleep too.

'What was I doing there?' said David. 'What was I in the middle of? Do you know? I was doing something important. Did you see me putting something together?'

'Two and two to make a daisychain?' said Keith. 'I don't know. I don't do dream things, do I?'

'I can't remember what it was,' said David. 'The hands of my memory go numb.'

'No one knows, if you don't,' said Keith. 'You were standing about in the cave. I rescued you. I thought it was a good habit, rescuing people, make them grateful, thank you and that.'

'It was four months between that lightning strike and coming home in the snow,' said David. 'I must have done something in the time. I was busy in the cave, and I want to finish whatever it was.'

Keith had heard enough, and was getting ready to write his next words for tomorrow's school.

'The leaf started the memory again,' said David. 'Something reached me in the cave and I was doing what it wanted when you rescued me. Tonight it felt like happening again. And you heard it.'

The house door opened, then the door of the room. Kirstie came in with brisk outside air round her, to collect Lyddy.

Lyddy dribbled. Keith said, 'And the leaf was trying to get your attention?'

'The thing that wants me has to attract attention through something,' said David, lifting the baby up and handing it over. 'Kirstie, here she is. Keith observed some strange behaviour. From his point of view it was rational. From mine it was invisible.'

'She stood up on her own,' said Keith, 'without any help; she was thinking of walking about.'

'Well, who's a clever bairn?' said Kirstie.

'Eef,' said Lyddy. Keith was pleased to hear his name. Even babies can flatter you.

'It's time David went,' said Keith. 'I understand Lyddy, but I don't know what he's talking about.'

'Och,' said Kirstie, 'nonsense runs in the family like the second sight or haunted battlements.'

Keith's mother was in the room now too, drawing the curtains, because curtains are for drawing.

'Is it a mouse?' she said, her hand on the cord.

'Look, Lyddy, a mousikie,' said Kirstie

The leaf, crumpled soft with rain, crouched against the glass, ready to slink off in the wind.

'Cats will get it,' said Dr Wix. 'Town foxes.'

'Oh,' said Keith, matters solved for him with one word, one

memory of brown backs in the grass turned from terror to wild life. 'Foxes, of course.'

'I'll walk home,' said David. 'Blow away the cobwebs.'

'Just thoughts,' said Keith.

When David turned for home at the bottom of the market square, leaning into the wind to stride the better, he saw the town lights go out in a wave, their reflections drying brittle on the cobbles at his feet a thousandth of a second after them.

He was walking on grass, as if he had walked into a field; or a new place altogether, with dry night about his head. He came to a climax of perception, seeing things afresh, new, and deep.

Tonight's stars were random bright, their rocket-trail spanning a vapoury sky. There was a rising moon, brightly full, couched on its halo.

There were no houses. The castle had not been built yet. Or had fallen down, David considered.

He knew that this moment was not happening now, or to him at all, but was like remembrance after many years. More years than I have had, David thought. I can't go back so far.

He remembered, as if he had experienced, the broad silken wings of the machine lifting and spreading, pushing and stroking the air, the sense of leaving the surface, a continuous thrill of movement; of being alone, a machine flying itself.

Meaningless meanings poured into his mind: these were recollections he could not have. He held the flask of chrono-leptons ready to drop them in the sea to decay back to datum. They interacted with time and should not have been recreated.

I do not know the words, David thought, for himself. I did

not do it, he thought on behalf of another consciousness. I am to spend my day disposing of them, and may not be back in time for tonight's sky games.

Chrono-leptons were hard enough for David to understand; the sky games had a surround of meaning, nothing actual at all. (David saw for a moment the lights swinging behind the clouds, heard the plunging fall of a contestant, joined the rattling of applause round the mountains, remembering the past of something trying to tell him about its present long ago or far ahead; the chrono-leptons interfering with that.) He felt the sense, but no detail.

Stars wheeled overhead. This was flight, the history of another event. Wings rippled.

Butterfly, David thought, his eyes dwelling on the bright fluctuating patterns. It was his own thought, translated from another eye, because there was no butterfly. The understanding brought David back to himself. As if that thought had caused it, the stars twisted violently. The container of chrono-leptons fell away from his hands . . . from what he held them with . . . but this was not the history of his own limbs, which had appeared round him, assembled instantly into local reality.

'You all right, Wix?' someone was saying. 'Stepping off the kerb like that.' Dr Tate looked back from a stopped car that had been passing. 'You'll have to stop dreaming, Wix, if you're going to get anywhere in this world. Alive, that is.'

Then he had gone. A limp dead leaf flew against David's face, and away again, like a messenger with his delivery over. What it meant was still unclear.

Later on, Keith with his room light still on heard his mother tap scrapily like a long-legged thing in the grass, turned the light off and knew that what surrounded the house were not foxes and, in spite of all, slept in the dark.

EIGHT

'Molasses, jauping,' said Nellie Jack John, opening the cab door of the International and looking down on David and Keith. They met him above Swang, crossing the lane from Crackpot to town. 'T' yowes lick it up. It's gitten that modern vittle stuff in. Get by, Jip.' He brushed the dog's tail from his face.

Jip was wanting to stay in the cab for the ride, and equally wanting to jump out and rampage in the morning's snow round David and Keith. Dog breath and grin steamed out of the open door.

'Daft about it,' said Nellie Jack John, 'is yowes.' He was taking a drum of molasses, packed between square bales of hay in the tractor box, to sheep on the moor. The molasses slopped sulkily in the drum – jauping.

'Vitamins,' said Keith.

'Sike ket,' said Nellie Jack John, meaning, 'Some such rubbish'.

'We'll shut the gates,' said David. The gates were opposite each other on either side of the lane.

'Nay, there's no stock out,' said Nellie Jack John. 'Leave them – I'll be back down from yonder sharpish.'

He went on up the lane, following a set of tracks already there, the tractor box swaying behind him. White smoke rose from the chimney, turning to grey against thin snow on the ground.

'He's been up already,' said David. 'I mean he's already been this way, but he can't have.'

'How do they eat it?' Keith was wondering aloud.

'They're got one spoon between them, idiot,' said David, not thinking about it. 'They hand it round.'

'We could look,' said Keith. 'But Gibraltar . . .'

They were walking down to Keith's house to tackle together the War of the Spanish Succession, which had been so important for those people then, and for Dr Tate now. He wanted David to prove that England had no right to Gibraltar, and Keith to prove that England had every right. It would suit their characters, he said. They could blame the French this week, and the Dutch next week, and the Common Market a few days later. 'It's all in there,' he had said. 'Then and now, no different, not causing each other, but inevitably connected.'

'Gibraltar can wait,' said David. 'Common Market, and all this funny money.' Seeing the sheep eat molasses was more important, but inevitably connected. They followed the tractor up the hill.

'One set of tracks going up,' said David. 'One coming down. He must have come back another way when he went up first.'

'You jump to conclusions,' said Keith. 'I make certain of each step of the way.'

After the War of the Spanish Succession was dealt with, and

exams were over, and if Keith had done well, he was to leave school and start work in his father's office, where legal things were right, connected, and inevitable.

'I shall be an archaeologist,' said David. 'They are only allowed to guess.'

He stood in the snow, looking up the hill to the allotment wall, and down to where the fields lay scattered with snow down to Swang Farm, the lingering drifts against the walls the negative shadow of winter. The farm was having coal put on its fire, and thick smoke hurtled from the chimney.

'The tractor we just saw go up here,' said David, 'is now going into the yard down there. I'd know it anywhere.'

The red International stopped in the yard. The engine rattled to a halt. The driver got out, and the dog, and the door dropped back. Seconds later the two noises climbed the hill, the engine clatter ending, and the snecking twang of the door. The dog barked and ran about the yard. The faint cluck of the house door closing walked separately up the hill.

'He's still up here,' said Keith. 'I can hear him. Everybody has old Internationals. Cab doors wear out first.'

'Farm dogs look the same,' said David

'But they're not all called Jip,' said Keith, and looked worried, because that was not at all his sort of joke.

The tractor they had met was still roaming the allotment. Sheep were calling and coming to it. When David led the way through the moor gate the tractor engine had stopped and the sheep were no longer calling. There was a rich smell of molasses, which had been poured into wooden troughs, then eaten at once, with energetic licking still discovering the taste in cracks in the troughs.

Sheep, licking their lips, gathered round David and Keith, hoping all visitors brought sweeties.

'Well,' said David, 'been there, done that, should have worn the T-shirt, it's cold enough.'

Keith was walking back the way they had come, along the marks of the tractor wheels. 'He's been up, and come down,' he said. 'But where is he? We should have seen him on his way down.'

'He's gone on to more sheep somewhere else,' said David. 'We'll go back and do nice warm Gibraltar and the War of the Liquorice Sticks.'

'I can only taste molasses,' said Keith, after a pause for rapid thinking, and venturing on a joke. 'I'd nearly forgotten liquorice is called 'spanish' by children. But it wasn't Nellie Jack John going into the farmyard. Impossible!'

'No,' said David. 'But you know about impossible – it happens more often than probability allows. Like your wit.'

They walked beyond the troughs to where the tractor had left traces of fallen oil black as molasses, among the scuffle of dog's paw marks and Nellie Jack John's boot prints. Up the hill from this trample a skein of tyre tracks trod rough grass and crusting snow with distinct treads, so recent that grass was still lifting and recovering, and the sedge called seaves straightening its rod-like leaves.

'No snow yesterday,' said Keith. 'Even up here. It must have been today.'

'He didn't have time to do this,' said David. 'And he never came down past us.'

The tracks diverged. One set, narrow front tyres and broad rear wheelmarks, went left, another right.

'Going up,' said David. 'Making a loop. Coming down. I'll go right.'

'Coming up,' said Keith. 'Going down.'

A hundred yards further on, the track David had followed stopped, broad tyres and narrow ending together. 'There's nothing beyond,' David called back to Keith. 'Unbroken snow. The front wheels and the back wheels get to exactly the same line and stop. Impossible.'

'Wind,' said Keith. 'A snow shower covered it. It's just a very cold day.' He wanted to get away from here and be by the fire, even with the War of the Spanish Succession. He did not want to consider the impossible.

Behind him, something in the molasses made the sheep belch. He turned to look, to make sure only sheep stood there.

'Just go on a b . . .' David was saying. His words were nipped off, like the tractor tracks.

Keith turned to him, to retrieve lost words spoken in another direction.

David was not there. He had quietly gone, this time with no flash of darkness, no cry welcoming what was beyond, no farewell – nothing. The hillside was empty, snow greying to a grey sky.

NINE

The strangeness was obviously caused by the angle of the sun, the way light fell on the snow in the hollows, flattening the surface to an almost colourless bruise. And some tilt in the day itself seemed to have lifted one end of the landscape a little.

Between lifting one foot and setting it down again not quite where he expected, David's leg had been jarred, his teeth bitten his tongue, his head adjusted to a new skyline.

His eyes could not read the random embroidery on the counterpane of snow, a new world under its opaque cover.

'It is an optical illusion,' he called back to Keith. 'Keith.' He rubbed snow on his tongue. Keith did not reply. Keith was not there.

Half a stride beyond where the tractor tyre-marks had been curiously snapped off complete in an impossible way, David found himself in another place, not on the hillside above Vendale.

Yet it was that hillside too. Sheep were absent, but the scene was the same without them, and without Keith. The trail of the tractor began again under his feet, starting abruptly where it had left off, the earlier end becoming the new beginning, sudden, illogical. All four wheels do not reach the same terminus, or start again together: there should be the length of the wheelbase between them. Yet all the wheelmarks had ended the same distance along the track, and now all began from the same place.

David knew that the world he inhabited was still underfoot, a pace away. He dared not think otherwise. He also knew that while he saw a different world, what he felt was not his own state.

Though he was apparently alone, another's distant sorrow hung round him. Another heart was desolate, far from a different place and time. David had not lost his own world, nor was longing for a different one. This is not me, he thought. These are the thoughts of another mind. I do not know this other place it is remembering.

Another person was weeping in him, thinking through him, lost, and speaking to him.

It was terror and joy, relief and regret, disbelief and conviction. David felt sensations as if they were his own, though he knew they were strangers that had been squatting in his mind unseen for years, speaking after an interval that felt longer than his life so far.

'I am listening,' he said. The words were difficult to say, as if speech had not happened here before, air did not know what to do with it, and words were meaningless because grammar had no experience. Something spoke directly to his mind, without words coming between. He was being begged to respond, pleaded with for help.

There was a picture. David had been running along a street . . . no, the other one had been running, and not along a street, but a radius . . . This world's explanations were translating another's.

Running, but not getting away. He had to stop, and accept the work given to him. Not for long, he was told; do this for us and be home tomorrow. His own family, David felt, the other person's own family. Not my family, he knew; not anything I can understand. I am being sent a picture of a picture, degraded by incomprehension, a Chinese whisper.

He heard the turmoil of ideas coming from technicians getting the journey ready. The task was simple, a child could do it; simple, but confidential; not to be left to anyone picked off the street.

An automatic flight, programmed. At a certain point the load would be released, and the machine return. There was nothing to do but sit. If anything went wrong help would come.

David heard these things inside him, like a compact disc game with all responses and reactions latent, but not knowing what screen button to press.

There were elements (simpler than helium and hydrogen) that no longer existed (like lawrencium), formed at the creation. Now they had been artificially made again, a few atoms in a flask, chrono-leptons, particles of time.

'Active,' David's mind heard. 'They strain probability, possibility, and the laws of the growing universe and must not exist.'

I don't understand, David told himself. I can't learn meaning from it.

A crystal jar, like something made of petals, held the chrono-leptons, discernible like fireflies deep inside it, yet beyond.

The flying machine had moving bright wings, a tame creature, ready to fly.

'The poison is time,' David heard, like the quick tongue of a dream reaching for you as your eyes close, with meanings beyond analysis.

What he had heard began to fade in the strained reality of sunlight on the moor; and something like a shout in his head faded and wailed. There had been a gap in what David was being told. The person speaking had jumped along his narrative, and wanted to speak more directly.

The person was there, in the grass of the moor, under the sparse heather, watching.

'Too small,' it said, in David's mind again. But it was talking too fast, too deeply. Words and meanings and structure and interface separated into different things with no links between them, yet garbled.

The thing behind it all became large, and visible, rising out of the ground, standing as tall as David, but wider and enormous. It spoke. It was not a word, only the rustling of its jaws or limbs, ending in a leathery rattle.

David was being drawn into the mind of this thing, and he struggled against it. He could not allow himself to be transformed against his will. The other mind's eagerness to talk made it noisy, but dumb and threatening. There was a name for it, a simple name, but David could not recall words now.

He stepped away. His heel caught again on a different angle of ground. Vendale was round him once more, and sheep were on the hill, more real for having been absent, still licking cracks in the wooden troughs for sweet stuff.

Keith stood on his last footprints by the end of the tractor tracks. He looked in David's direction, walked backwards, fell over, picked himself up, and ran away.

David understood. He had come back as the wider and enormous thing he had seen, into whose thoughts he had been drawn. But the impression lasted on his mind only the length of time it took to think it. He came back across the line between two realities and was himself again, two arms, two legs, voice, and upright body. The other thing dwindled away.

Keith was running, and looking back, among startled sheep. 'Wait on,' David called, the words coming out clogged and foreign, as if his mouth were full of hair, no, something finer than hair, like undissolving candy floss. 'Wait, Keith.'

Keith stopped running and came back up the hill warily. 'It was the mist,' he said. 'I didn't know what was coming out of it.'

'Me,' said David. 'What did you see?'

'Bloody great spider,' said Keith, being wildly calm, in control of his panic, but still having it.

'That's all right then,' said David, glad to learn that they had both seen it. 'I was a bit moody, that's all, just sort of thinking. We'd better go on and do that War of the Spanish Succession homework.'

'You were a spider,' said Keith. 'Attercop.'

'No,' said David. He knew what was what. 'Something thought I was one. I was thinking through a spider. Attercop as big as me. I don't know why. Made you swear, anyway.' He spoke clearly now, his mouth no longer full of web. 'Attercop on the job.'

The sheep followed David and Keith to the allotment gate, with accusing bleats and uncomplimentary stamping of the feet.

'It'll be better sorted,' said David, looking at tractor tracks. 'How long was I this time?'

'Didn't miss you,' said Keith. 'You weren't out of sight long enough for me to notice until you began to come back.'

'That's what I thought,' said David.

'Get it settled,' said Keith. 'There'll be a reason, even if it's only insanity.'

'We were there,' said David. 'Just look at the tractor tracks, will you.'

Beyond the allotment gate, their own uphill prints of heel and toe overlaid those of the tractor.

'It has been down once and up once,' said David. 'We saw John down at Swang while we still heard him at the top. Look at the tracks. That front tyre pushed the grass down that way, so it must have been going up the hill. But this tyre goes over the other set of tracks, which proves that the tractor came down the hill *before* it went up it. We saw it back at Swang before it got to the top. We heard it there. We know he was there. The tracks already on the ground when he went up the hill must have been the tracks of him coming down afterwards. Because we didn't see him, did we?'

'He made them another day,' said Keith, sure there was an answer outside mere impossibility.

'It only snowed today,' said David. 'The tractor crossed into another time. John Cherry was there a length of time and came out earlier, so the length of time must have been a minus quantity.'

'We're all right,' said Keith. He was glad to be certain of that. Or at any rate nearly certain. 'Aren't we?'

'We don't know,' said David. 'Out here in this grassy lane, it may be us that's wrong again.'

'It'll just be you, as usual,' said Keith.

'Shut up,' said David. 'Listen.'

A town church clock chimed, chimed, chimed again, and again, and then rang out the slow hours.

'It should be eleven,' said David, between strokes. 'Someone thinks they know.'

'A machine,' said Keith. 'Called a clock.'

David waited for the last long pause after the eleventh stroke, and heard nothing more.

'Eleven,' Keith said, a finger short of the total.

'Which day?' David wondered. 'Which year?'

Panic was over, but left a hollow place. To fill it they went down the hill in the quickest way, rolling childishly over and over in the snow. Keith hit a hump and finished in a running spring. Sensible cold water ran down his neck. David put his racing head into a solitary gorse bush. Realistic spines and grating bark were part of welcome actuality.

They both sat in the snow, bruised, damp, and even bleeding, and both decided that both sides of Spain had lost both sides of the War of Succession for the day, so there was nothing to write about.

Below the lane, at Swang, the red tractor started up again. The dog ran after it, jumped in the box, and took charge of operations from there.

'Normality,' said Keith.

'We'll let the liquorice allsorts look after themselves for a day,' said David. 'Dr Tate can buy his own Gibraltar rock.'

They met Nellie Jack John by a gate above the farm, bringing in logs from a stricken oak tree.

'You came down before you went up,' said Keith. 'With molasses.'

'Aye,' said Nellie Jack John, unsurprised. 'If thou meets Attercop, thou must gan home sharpish.'

'Attercop,' said David. 'Do you see him much?'

'T' moor-booger?' said Nellie Jack John. 'Oft eneugh. Today I'd to gan on for some yowes that'd gitten themselves trapped yonder. Yonder, some part, 's where he lives. Nowt to do wi' us. I'll get him yah day. I promised that soldier fellow.'

'Just a word,' said Keith, keeping it that way. 'Attercop.' In some ways knowing large spiders were real and not imaginary made them less horrifying. You can block up doorways and keep the light on, but the mind stays unfenced and in the dark.

'Grand skin for a drum, Attercop,' said Nellie Jack John. 'If Attercop meets me that's a different tale.'

AMONGHANDS

ONE

Gytrash had not yet worked out how to drive the quad. He was happy to sit on it and wait for Lyddy to do that. Then he would leap off and attack the wheels. Other times he would sit and watch them for unruly behaviour, taking charge for whole afternoons at the gate two miles away by the road, until Lyddy came out from school, started up, and drove herself home. Going and coming, Lyddy ignored any parent, or brother, who brought a car to the gate.

'He's only sort of months old,' said Lyddy. 'Which is sort of the same as me, if you're a dog. He'll be doing half days at school next term.'

She had had him a year; or they had had each other: it was hard to tell, dog years or girl years.

Nellie Jack John had come across her tumbling about the moor edge, as if she were fighting, but without an opponent, shrieking and triumphant after beating off the invisible assailant, and emerging with the damp parchmenty purse that was Gytrash, in his skin and little else.

'He didn't want to come,' Lyddy had said, looking at her bitten thigh, giving Nellie Jack John the bundle to hold, taking off her torn cardigan and swaddling the damp sac of puppy in it. 'He got bigger and badder, but I knew. I *let* him bite me.'

'Thou's gitten t'Gytrash,' said Nellie Jack John, thinking about it and naming a legendary demon dog. 'I heard t'Gytrash had generally-what gitten folk, not folk gitten him, like riving their heads off.'

'That's his name,' Lyddy said. 'Tell me again so I can come when he calls.'

'Get thou in the tractor box,' said Nellie Jack John. 'Tha'd best take yon thing home wi'thee.'

Dr Wix had made a list of things wrong with the limp bundle when Lyddy brought it home in her cardigan. Three cardigans ago, Kirstie said before long, knitting another and another, as Lyddy and Gytrash destroyed them. 'Four.'

Lyddy had laughed at this expenditure of maternal effort.

'In stitches,' said David. 'Plain, purl.' But Lyddy did not do jokes that only had to be said.

'It's got hypothermia,' said Dr Wix. 'Jaundice, worms, distemper, hard pad, worms, mange, canker, lice, worms, squint, fleas, smell, spots, puke and runny poos, starvation, and neonatal deprivation.'

'Daddy,' said Lyddy, 'you mean it's dead?'

'No,' said Dr Wix. 'Its mother threw it away. Very sensible of her, I think, Lyddy. Seems to be all right otherwise, apart from a touch of rabies, which it probably caught from you, like his habit of piddling on my knee.'

'Called Gytrash,' said Lyddy, bringing him into the family by naming him.

'I see we get to keep it,' said Kirstie. 'Poor wee thing.'

'You kept me,' said Lyddy. 'And I was a girl. This is a boy.'

'I only listed the negative aspects,' said Dr Wix. 'They were all I could find. Did I mention worms?'

That was a year ago. At the price, Kirstie said, of a pedigree Saluki, which she herself would have preferred, Gytrash had been kept alive and cured of all those things, and others too, some of them the first cases within living memory.

'He's too well,' Kirstie would say. 'I'm not sure he doesn't glow in the dark.'

Gytrash had spent that first year practising to live up to his name, tearing bits off Lyddy, sharpening his teeth on her, ripping her skin, pulling her hair out, and destroying her clothes. He had turned into a tall rangy brindled dog with broad shoulders, likely to throw strangers about in a playful way, and deal with family members as if they were equals.

Today Gytrash had not seen David for nearly two weeks, because David had been away on a course, and had thrown him about for a time, but been ignored.

'Take him a leg off,' said Lyddy, admiringly.

Gytrash had only spilled a mug of tea and ragged a button off a shirt and made a hole in a shoe. For Gytrash that counted as inactivity or benevolence.

'He likes you,' said Lyddy. 'You should be glad. If he hated you, you would be dead. But he's trained to like people.'

Gytrash sat on his rump wagging it and his tail, and grinned round a pole that David was trying to put into the Land Rover.

'He doesn't get enough company,' said David. 'Living out

here in the wilderness.' Crackpot Hall was alone and distant, away up the hillside. David thought no other house looked towards it, except through lavatory windows.

'There's me,' said Lyddy. 'I'm company enough.'

'True,' said David, winning the pole back, closing the door, wiping his dog-slathered hands on the grass. 'You're just right for him. I'll see you, Lyddy.'

'You haven't told me where you're going,' said Lyddy. 'So how can you see me there?'

'I mean I'll be back for tea,' said David. 'Or before that if it rains, unless I go in at Swang to see Eileen and Frank and Nellie Jack John. Until then I'm measuring at the Jingle Stones. When I come back you can help me put the measurements into the computer.'

'You can read out the co-ordinates,' said Lyddy. 'I'll write them in.' She knew about that at school. 'One hundred, one hundred, two hundred, two hundred. That's a square. Or a circle. Kiss me.'

David bit her nose.

'Kiss Gytrash,' said Lyddy.

Gytrash bit David's nose.

TWO

David drove down along Vendale to Swang Farm, and past it, parking beside the Jingle Stones. He walked down to the farm, to see if it was convenient for him to go to the stones. Borrowing the key, Eileen had said, when the school came, baffling Dr Tate. Dr Tate usually assumed that he saw everything, and that if he had not, then someone else was being illogical.

David had to look twice at Eileen when she came to the door. He was not sure that the diminished person he saw was indeed Eileen. She has aged, he thought. My father would know.

'You called it getting the key,' he reminded her.

'And welcome,' Eileen said. 'You don't need to ask, David, I'm sure. But come in, even if it's just for a minute; there's the teapot warm and ready so you'll have a cup.'

David went in and sat against the familiar fire, with his feet on the same rug, and nothing changed since last time, smell of polish on wood, wisps of coal and wood smoke from tar bogies under the kettle that hung on the reckon over the fire; the hint of farm animals from Frank's chair that he sat in. Something creaked and tapped in the ceiling overhead. David looked up.

'They won't waken,' said Eileen, water sparkling from kettle to teapot. 'If he's been listening he'll know everything, but not what to do about it, and if it's her, she's just being family.'

'Him?' said David, whispering so that he would not disturb it, 'Her? The boggarts?'

'The pair of them,' said Eileen, stirring the teapot. There had been two boggarts for several years now.

'Never mind them, are you all right, Eileen?' asked David. Eileen was not the well-waxing farmer's wife that David remembered and expected, allowing for the fact that people and things grow less large across time. She had shrunk and shrivelled, her eyes seemed clouded, and her movements were less sure and automatic. She had to peer a little at the teapot, and take another hand to the kettle.

'Middling,' said Eileen. 'There's nowt, like, wrong – diseases, or such. Fretted a bit, that's all, and I've lost weight and gone into less room.'

'You have,' said David. 'You don't sound like yourself. Is it that new doctor giving you the wrong stuff?'

'Since your Dad retired I haven't needed anything,' said Eileen. 'I'm well of myself, but the lease is on my mind.'

'Lease?' said David, enquiringly, not knowing quite what Eileen meant. But he recalled that Frank went into the town regularly to pay the rent, which of course meant that he did not own the farm. 'I did know that, but it never came to my mind. I really thought that Swang belonged to you.' He further remembered slowly the time the school had been here, when Eileen had said she might not be here next time, for reasons that meant nothing to David then.

'No,' said Eileen. 'Swang doesn't belong to us. We thought it would be here for John to have when we've done, and he could live here. We've paid the rent on the very dot all these years, and it seemed sure that John could take over – like set, and bound to be. Frank's been a good tenant, and John would follow just as good. He knew farming when he came to us. We wouldn't mind living in the town, if we still had a part, like if John got wed. Frank could drive up and help, and that. But Swang is part of us, and if we have to lose it to strangers it would be like our heart got taken away.'

Eileen, now before David's eyes, had changed, and so did David's view of how people lived on the land they worked. He was silent a moment, working things out. 'Keith's father will help you,' he said at last, when Eileen gave him the mug of tea.

'It was Mr Heseltine that had to tell us,' said Eileen. 'He came with Keith, because Keith's looking into things for us. The lease runs out at the turn of the century, and Swang's in a trust, and no one knows who the trust belongs to, so he can't ask about it, and they don't know what to do about it, or whether we can stop here, or owt. I thought you'd know all about that, David, being around with Keith so much.'

'Keith can't tell me things,' said David. 'Not now he's working in the office. And I don't see him so much, either. Is it because you adopted John? Would that make a difference? But what will you do? You and Frank. Nellie Jack John can work anywhere, so it's not so bad for him.'

'It'll be right, David,' said Eileen. 'It's nowt to do with how

John came to us.' She gave the fire a dose of coal slack and changed the subject. 'I mustn't load you with our troubles, David. Now, I haven't seen your sister in a bit; is she all right? And your dad; it doesn't seem the same now he's retired and not the doctor any more: it makes you feel not quite well all the time but not daring to get worse. And Sister Mackenzie, she'll be busier than ever with the business to run, and being your sister's mother?'

'And mine,' said David. 'Part time.'

Eileen poured tea, sat down and relaxed a little, offered parkin, and pushed a cup to David. 'You won't disturb anything up at the stones, David? The men are at market, John with some beasts, Frank to pay his rent. He's always done it the day before it's due, except one time in the snow, and Mr Heseltine backdated the receipt. They'll be home for their dinners, so come by and see them when you've done. Is it going to rain? Have you been home?'

'They're all well,' said David, answering the rest of the questions, or remarks, in one. 'And I'm only doing some measuring. I've been on a course about it. So that's all I'll do now.' He drank tea. It used to be mugs, but now he was a visitor, not just a bairn coming in and out, so the cup sat in a saucer with a spoon, and there was a plate for his square of parkin.

'Measuring?' said Eileen. 'Our stones? You can measure, but you can't count how many there are, except at midsummer.'

'I didn't know there was a day you could,' said David. 'I only heard that you couldn't. I was going to disprove it.'

'It's midsummer day tomorrow,' said Eileen. 'Frank's paying his rent a day early. Wait while tomorrow, there may be more stones today than you know, David. They're there for a purpose. Be careful.'

'I will,' said David. Then they were talking about David's other sister, Clare, who had not been his sister at all, but had been wished on him, then given to him. She had lived at Swang, and died there gently, in the front bedroom upstairs, and her ashes put in the orchard.

'We thought she would be there for ever,' said Eileen. 'Poor little mite. Will the next people bother?'

Over their heads something moved in the ceiling, beside the long kitchen beam. Ashes were in the orchard, but something had stayed in the house, alive, alert, able to run and climb and jump out of trees. Dr Tate had once said the right thing about that, thinking he was talking about Queen Mary and the loss of Calais. *Dimidium animae* had been his words; half of her soul; and that had stayed, not as a ghost, but as something else.

'Boggarts,' said Eileen. 'They walk up and down the stairs at night, but we take no notice, it's just laiking. The orchard's lovely, David.'

David had not been there in a long time. That false but pitiable sister had been supplanted by Lyddy, who needed no allowances made for her.

'I'll go there,' he said, remembering when they had put her ashes by, and something had run away and climbed a tree and fallen from it clumsily and joyously for the first time.

The garden had been flooded with flowers, and at

midsummer they were deep and fresh, and blackbirds were keeping guard. The ashes were under a stone. David stood by it for a minute. Eileen scolded some dandelions and a tangle of goose-grass. A robin chirruped when it sprang down to the disturbed soil.

'You don't know what to think,' said Eileen.

'I couldn't come back easily,' said David, 'because at first it was the only sister I'd ever had, called Clare. Then when Lyddy was born she was the real one, and I couldn't remember anyone else.'

'The mother,' said Eileen, shaking her head, 'well, she brought the bairn up to think she was your sister, just to give her away.'

'She trained her,' said David. 'Lyddy was never trained. She just grew up to be herself.'

'They do,' said Eileen.

'But that's all right,' said David.

'That time,' said Eileen. 'When she came here, just a little mite, not four years old.'

Kirstie had explained to Lyddy that Clare, who might have been her sister, rested here, with a mouse called Muz who had belonged to David, and who could run about better than Clare and not fall off the edge of the table.

'And dance?' Lyddy wanted to know. 'How can I know my sister?'

Neither of them could dance, Kirstie said, and Lyddy had looked to David to confirm that it was true.

Then, before the stone that covered Clare's ashes, she had danced for them both, to an inner music. And gradually, others had invisibly joined in so that the grass swung and moved in three places.

'The cats,' said Lyddy. 'Eileen's cats are dancing too.'

She had danced herself to sleep. Her legs had given way at last, and David had carried her away. The two boggarts of Swang had jostled beside him then banged their way up under the bedroom floor above the kitchen.

At the garden gate, on this later day, Eileen wrapped her hands in her apron and watched David across the yard and up the hill.

THREE

David went up the fields to the moor edge, as high as Crackpot Hall again. In the warm day the cool flow of memory wrinkled his back. It is longer ago for me, he thought, than it will ever be for Eileen. She has remembered better.

There was rain looming over the fells to the west, but so far nothing falling to the ground. But it was coming. At first he could see Crackpot Hall, two miles away, then the air grew damp and dense and made the hills one colour, blotting out a house made of the very stone of the hills.

At the Jingle Stones he fetched a post from the Land Rover, and drove it into the ground, hitting with a mallet. Echoes came back from the surrounding stones, and hung about in the still air. Sheep and their lambs came to look, snatch at bristly grass, and go away chewing triumphantly.

'You can count them,' said David to himself, looking round. The stones were so real they must be numerable. A sheep answered, 'No-o-o.'

He walked round the circle. There were twenty-three stones, one or two of them fallen, and one missing, which was now a gatepost at Swang Farm.

Or twenty-four? Did I start with this one or add it on at the end? David wondered. He stayed where he was and ran his eye round the circle.

He lost count in a slow flicker. He could not reliably scan from stone to stone and count every one once, and not count some of them twice. The calculation always went astray, as if his eyes stopped working properly. But looking in that way was not measuring. Measuring would settle matters. He began to set out a baseline inside the circle.

Nearby sheep began to look uneasily about them. They picked up their own lambs with a glance, and led them away. A moment later David heard shouts. At first he thought it was Eileen, on some inexplicable errand with sheep, but it was a higher voice. He decided it must be a school party walking the hills.

I will be totally methodical and professional, he decided. And ignore them.

A drop of rain fell on his cheek. There was the noise of an engine. David knew now what it was, before it came in sight, because running ahead was Gytrash, making for him, and about to romp once more.

Tess of the Baskervilles, he said to himself.

Gytrash picked up the surveying tape first, tied elaborate knots in it, and shook it until it died. He then swallowed loops of it.

The quad, with Lyddy riding as usual on tip toe, bottom up, head down, came between two stones into the ring. Lyddy was shouting at Gytrash, and at David.

'I tried to make him stay at home,' she said. 'But he won't listen. I came along the lane and through the fields, and a watersplash, a big dub. I know the way, and I've been here before.' She had mud on her face, hair flying, and no helmet. 'I've been further than this, and I know the way there too.'

'You'd better go back before it rains,' said David, pulling tape out of Gytrash, winding it wet back on its reel. 'Does Mum know where you are?'

'I didn't tell her,' said Lyddy. 'She'll know I'm with you.'

'You aren't,' said David. 'You should go home. You aren't being helpful, Lyd.'

'Of course I am,' said Lyddy.

'Why don't you go down to Swang?' said David. 'Eileen would like to see you. She was just asking about you.'

'You just want me to go away,' said Lyddy.

'I wish you would go away,' said David. 'In case you haven't got the message.'

The rain began now. In seconds Gytrash was careering round the circle with water spraying from his heels. Lyddy shouted at him, drawing her cardigan round her and shivering.

'Go away, Lyddy,' said David. 'Lydia, Lydia.' She was called that in moments of extreme nuisance. 'Go to Eileen, sit beside the fire. I'll collect you later. Or something.'

Lyddy wrinkled her face. She was here, which was a fact that continued. She set off to chase Gytrash down, a game that usually ended with Gytrash chasing the quad and biting tyres, and a crash of some sort.

The quad swung across the middle of the circle, to get

alongside Gytrash. Then Lyddy aimed it, and drove it between two of the standing stones. There was a flicker of light, a sudden gleam like the sun out of the wet clouds.

The quad, with Lyddy on it, went out of sight and hearing between the stones, and did not reappear. It and its rider did not go into mist, or rain, but out of existence. The noise died without warning, not fading but terminating. Where there had been echo there was solid silence, not even a ringing in David's ears. After the flicker of light the quad and its rider had no more presence.

Gytrash sniffed his way between two stones, trotted uneasily to David, stood by him, looked at the place where Lyddy had vanished, lifted his chin, and howled.

His tail drooped. He put down his muzzle, sniffed the grass, picked up a scent, and followed it, giving a groaning howl as he moved, to show that he considered himself lost. The scent led him to the same two stones.

Like Lyddy and the quad, he went out of perception between them with a flick of light, and his doleful moan went with him.

In the distance the sounds of the moorland, the calling of lambs, the whauping of the curlews, the whisperings of tiny becks in the peat, still made familiar sense.

The sky was hidden with a continuing flicker of darkness, and David felt himself hot and cold, faint with horror. Because Lyddy could never find her way back from that other place; that other place that David had forgotten about, having grown out of his visits there, no longer believing his recollections were true memory. That it was here, at these stones, he had never considered, until it now came to him fully that here was the likeliest place for such a boundary as he had once crossed into another field of time.

Where Attercop lived, Attercop that even the practical Nellie Jack John respected.

For the second time within half an hour a ripple brushed his back, but this time it was not regret and inadequacy that branded him, but the terror that what had visited him would return to visit Lyddy.

FOUR

The place David had been in must still exist, and in it would be whatever presence had come more than once to him in the past.

Alternatively Lyddy was still in her own ambience, and was at home in her real world, with David yonder where he had been before, years earlier. The tinkling of beck water and the calling of sheep would be the same in either place, and were no indication of unique familiarity.

But in the distance a tractor was firing up, and a moment later two low-flying Eurofighters scratched across the sky, contouring the fells, the hills shouting back the rasp of their engines. David was in his own environment. But where was Lyddy?

Probably at home, David told himself. She's got away. She drove off.

Or she might be reckless behind a rock, hiding, waiting to jump on him, without knowing what fears he had for her.

David went through on Lyddy's track, step by step, without being conscious of change until the riot of jets was all at once closed back into its box, their chromatic violent sound gone, the black sheet of silence all that showed.

The becks and little runnels babbled ceaselessly on, as they might have done at any time in history, recorded or not; wind rattled at David's ears; sheep called across the boundaries of another world in the universal sheep language. The day was dry, under a similar wind, and the sun was leaking through a bedraggled cloud in thin syrup.

Something had changed, whether by a day, an hour, a century, or a millennium; and this was the far side of reality, the place Nellie Jack John called yonder.

Yonder in time, David realised; but the same place.

Lyddy was not far inside. She had a friend her own size. They were sitting on the quad together. The friend was eating cold pop-tarts. Lyddy had a pocketful, brought from her day to this. She herself was having a gagging fit, and a piece of pop-tart jumped from her mouth. For a moment she looked miserable.

'I came through too quick,' she said. 'It makes me sick.'

'We should go back,' said David. 'Who's that?'

'It's Alec-Edward,' said Lyddy, recovering and having another nibble, pleased with the little squat boy, rough as heather, sharing her food. 'They're better cold. You can burn your mouth if they've been in the toaster. Don't tell Mum I got them, tell her you had them for breakfast.'

'Time to come home, Lyd,' said David, playing it gently, remembering about eating when you are on the other side and being lost for seven years. 'I wasn't home for breakfast. You shouldn't come here without saying.'

'I can't say,' said Lyddy. 'They aren't there when I do. Mostly whenever I come our house isn't there, so I can't. Alec-Edward lives here all the time. Nellie Jack John comes through here, that's how I know the way.'

David looked up the dale. A moment ago there had been too much drizzle or mist for him to see Crackpot. Now the air was clear, but the house was not there. It lay among the furrows and tips of old lead mines when it was visible, but the trenches and mounds themselves were not visible. This was a time before the lead mines and before the house.

'You should say before you come,' said David.

'I don't know till I get here,' said Lyddy.

'But you know the way back,' he said, to reassure Lyddy and even more to reassure himself. He had not known he would get here either, so he had only a small argument to use. 'Why not go and tell them?'

Lyddy gave him a look that meant she certainly knew the way back, and had used it many a time, so why bother to ask?

'So we'd better go,' said David. 'Home.'

Lyddy had not finished being here, and took no notice. She was busy talking to Alec-Edward.

'You could give me a backstep,' said David, hoping to distract her by hitching a lift.

'Walk,' said Lyddy, firmly, queen in her own country. 'Like you came in.'

'I don't know the way,' said David, because he was now outside the circle of Jingle Stones, and might have come between any pair of them anywhere along their ragged bite.

'Don't get it wrong,' said Lyddy. 'There's spiders. I mean the big one.'

'Attercop,' said Alec-Edward, his mouth full of crust and jam. 'T'big moor-booger 'at'll git thee.'

She'll learn language, was David's next thought, riding on the back of his other anxieties. But she always says what's in her throat, anyway.

'He's teaching me how to talk the same as they do here,' said Lyddy.

'I expect it's time he went home too,' said David. But he knew he lacked the skill of being persuasive and convincing to strange kids like Alec-Edward, and aliens like Lyddy.

'You don't have to look after me,' said Lyddy. 'I can go to Alec-Edward's house. There isn't a problem. Do you know, they don't have writing here? There isn't anything to read, so it doesn't matter. You can't read, can you, Alec-Edward.'

'Ah dawn't knaw,' said Alec-Edward. He didn't care. 'Ah niver saw no words.'

Lyddy was calling for Gytrash. He was roaming in the heather, looking for something, and was almost invisible against the stalks. He was almost invisible in his own right, because light shone through him, not just by the tendon of the hind leg above the ankle; but wherever he stood against the sky the light came through his sandy colour and only the brindle showed.

'He's laiting of himself,' said Lyddy.

'T'other yan's felted away,' said Alec-Edward.

None of this meant anything to David. though he

understood the words: 'Laiting' was searching, and 'Felted away' was hidden.

He wanted to pull Lyddy out of this place and back to her own time and land. But it would be a case of the blind leading the oblivious, and he had to wait.

Perhaps he'll eat something, thought David. Then we can get a Suzuki . . . no, that was the quad, Saluki, and please Kirstie.

Lyddy left the quad and went to retrieve Gytrash. David went with her, to be within grabbing distance, in case there was an obvious doorway home again. In the snow, once, there had been signs; but now, on the naked fell, there was nothing.

Gytrash was mewling like a cat round a patch of heather, wanting to catch what was there but not daring to, darting and backing, lifting his eyebrows, baffled by something.

'You'll have to leave it,' Lyddy was saying firmly. 'We've got one, you daft thing, and it's you already.'

Among the roots of the heather lay a naked rabbity thing, with eyes young from not being long open to its world. It looked like Gytrash when he had first been brought home by Lyddy. David said so.

'It is him,' Lyddy told David. 'That's him before I brought him back.' To Gytrash she said, 'No, we've got one. Leave it.'

'It'll die if we leave it,' said David. 'But we don't want another.'

'No,' said Lyddy. 'It isn't another one. It's the same one before he was Gytrash. I keep finding him. This is a long time ago, and I've got Gytrash, so he can't die, can you, Gytie?'

Gytrash gathered his courage and darted in to lick the scrap of skinny fur. But there was nothing there when his tongue

91

uncurled. The pup faded and dislimned as he got nearer to it. He could not understand this event, but Lyddy had no difficulty with it.

'See,' she said. 'That's what happens.'

'Right,' said David. 'I've seen it all. We'll go home, Lyddy, before we meet Attercop. Goodbye, Alec-Edward.'

The pop-tarts were finished. Alec-Edward licked his fingers and put them up his nose. Gytrash hoovered up a crumb. Lyddy looked round.

'See you, Alec-Edward,' she said, making up her mind. 'Come on, Gytie, race you, Davy. I thought you wanted a backstep.'

'Not on Death's Quad,' said David, because a backstep on the quad was all problems. A backstep behind Lyddy on anything was even more problems.

'O.K.,' said Lyddy, and started the engine. Then she drove forward, pulling back on the steering to lift the front wheels from the ground, scattering mud over David, and swinging wildly between standing stones.

Once more she disappeared. David found her a moment later, inside the circle, engine stopped, Gytrash very sober beside her, her face puckered up against driving rain.

'It's the wrong place,' she said. 'It sometimes is.'

'No it isn't,' said David. 'My poles are here, and the Land Rover.'

'Good,' said Lyddy, and stood by while David manhandled the quad into the back of the Land Rover. 'Once it was total night time, and Attercop.'

Gytrash rode the quad home.

'I told you we'd get back,' said Lyddy, at Crackpot Hall, undoing the back door.

'It's home all right,' said David, lifting the quad out. 'But it might not be us, that's all.'

'Oh well, it never is,' said Lyddy. 'You get used to it.'

'You haven't got to go there,' said David.

'It wasn't me,' said Lyddy. 'You just said.'

FIVE

David and Keith were playing a game they called rock chess, laid out on the almost-bare ground between the new garden at Crackpot and the arid ancient mine-workings. There was no board and there were no squares, and the rules were random at first, and then excitable after Lyddy had got into the game. The two kings were earthfasts and could not be moved.

'I'm threatening your queen with my boulder, or bishop,' said Keith, sitting down after the effort of moving it.

'Oh, is it my queen?' said David. 'I was going to take it and remove it from the board, with this rook or ravine.'

'Of course it's your queen,' said Lyddy. 'Look on the top of my head.'

Dr Wix was sitting in a deck chair drinking something tawny. The red sky cast blue shadows.

'I can't understand a word you fellows are playing,' he said.

'Chest,' said Lyddy. 'I'm a nipple.'

David and Keith had thought she might go away, to bed, or something, if they were deliberately incomprehensible and the rules made no sense. They had begun the game of rock chess, setting out large boulders on the rubble-strewn ground. All the rocks were the same colour, except for a few crystals of galena.

'Diamonds,' Lyddy had said, abandoning bedtime and joining in, wearing pawns in her hair and demolishing a perfectly good opening gambit Keith had devised with a couple of quoins and a highly lucky self-bored stone from an extinct watercourse.

The diamonds were the pawns of each side. There was a white chalk mark on all of David's pieces, including his queen, Lyddy. Otherwise no one knew which rock was which piece or whose side it was on. Lyddy liked the game better that way she said. She thought the rules were like a Sunday School hymn, because she liked those as well, without understanding either.

'It's meant to be all mineral,' said Keith, who had taken no notice of Lyddy ever since she came, to make her wild. 'But there's an animal in the middle.'

'Except for the vegetables,' said Lyddy, sitting in a queenly way on a bishop, then lying down in a knight's move in the middle of the board, still talking about whether she liked the game. 'I don't like vegetables but I'm a vegetarian and live on pudding and crisps.'

'If it was golf,' said Keith, when one of his pieces rolled away into a rut, 'that would be a bunker.'

'That's one of Alec-Edward's words,' said Lyddy. 'It's swearing.' She went to sleep in the slow twilight.

'She'll hear all sorts at school,' said Dr Wix. 'What did she mean? Kirstie, do you know Alec-Edward at the school? When I was in practice I knew all the babies before they had names, so I should still know anyone of school age.'

'I don't know,' said Kirstie. 'Why?'

'It's either swearing or golf,' said Dr Wix. 'I think I'd prefer swearing to bad habits.'

'I enjoy the good Scottish game,' said Kirstie. 'I'd take her to bed, but she'll come to no harm where she is for now.'

Lyddy watched with one eye while David and Keith manoeuvred the game so that she won but could not walk off the board, surrounded by huge rocks.

Gytrash wandered over, sniffed at Keith's line of stone men, did something disrespectful to his king, wagged his tail, and went to sleep again.

'That was treason,' said Keith.

'My guardian angel,' said Lyddy.

'I've left all my gear at the Jingle Stones,' said David. Lyddy stirred. 'I'll get it in the morning,' he said, noticing her intention to follow again.

The sun went behind the hills, but not far because this was the eve of midsummer.

'That's the horizon, not the skyline,' said Keith. 'So this is still day.'

'Not the horizon but still day,' David repeated, and Keith said the same again. They used the words as a mantra to drive Lyddy to sleep. Lyddy watched, wanting to speak but not finding opportunity. Then her eyes closed, and she was asleep.

A few more lines about the horizon confirmed the fact. 'Now I'll have to wake her,' Kirstie murmured. 'That's worse.'

David and Keith went to the Land Rover and coasted down the steep lane with no lights or engine. The engine started on the slope, but David left the lights off. They were on the long lane, not on a highway.

'No dog about,' said Keith.

'Didn't notice us,' said David.

'We used to walk,' said Keith. 'Miles and miles.'

'Bikes,' said David. 'Leagues on leagues.'

'It was big for us then,' said Keith. 'The world was small and our ideas were cosmological.'

'Cosmetic,' said David. 'We never got anywhere.'

'Except back home,' said Keith.

Towards midnight they came to the Jingle Stones. Down at Swang the lights were out. A dog called to them, and rattled its chain.

'Too dark to work,' said David. 'I had to put the quad in the Land Rover this morning, so I left my poles. They'll be safer at home.'

'Check,' said Keith, grasping a Jingle Stone round its middle as if he were moving it and still playing rock chess.

'Eileen was funny about them,' said David, not troubling to respond to Keith's jest. 'Remember when we came up to survey them with the school? And Eileen talked about giving Tate the key? Well, I said that this morning, and she said people had to be careful.'

'Yes,' said Keith, letting go of the stone. 'I'm only being frivolous. Disrespectful, really.'

'She talked about the lease,' said David. 'She thought you might have said something to me about it. She says it's a mess.'

'Can't tell you anything about it,' said Keith. 'Confidentiality.

Can't talk to people about office matters.'

'I know,' said David. 'I'm just telling you that it's getting to her and making her ill, nervous.'

'I'll go on with my Dad,' said Keith. 'That lease is a mess, when it comes to an end. We'll have to talk about something else, David. We're not even Eileen's lawyers, but the owners'. It's just that we can't leave Frank and Eileen without any help, and they won't talk to anyone else. So nothing to say, David.'

'Lyddy followed me on,' said David, changing the subject at once. 'Then she went out of sight.'

Keith stood still. 'Yes,' he said. 'You did that once. More than once. It's obviously a Wixian property, something that Wixes can do.'

David saw that he was about to make a joke, and started slow clapping.

'Shut up,' said Keith. 'It's Wixcraft, that's all.'

'But, going back to the last remark but one,' said David, 'I got her back. I was changing the subject, that's all, but it isn't so important as Eileen and the lease. Now I'll go back to Eileen, but other stuff, not the lease. Eileen said about only counting the stones accurately on Midsummer Day. It's just going to be midnight, and not at all dark, and now we're here we could check the number. Superstition.'

'Definitely superstition,' said Keith. 'But we've had things worse than that, and we don't want to do them again, so let's go home. Things talking to us. Remember?'

'We were children,' said David. 'Then.'

'Now we're idiots,' said Keith. 'Is that the last pole? Let's be going, David. I don't want Attercop – it's like a hallucination.'

'It isn't midnight yet,' said David. 'We'll just do a rough count of stones. Two counts, one before and one after.'

'From outside,' said Keith. 'Sitting in the Land Rover outside the circle. Safer.'

'O.K.' said David. 'At the moment we're still here. I can see lights at the house. Probably brat going to bed.'

There was one little glow at Crackpot Hall. No other light showed anywhere. Perhaps there was a loom of streetlights towards the town, but with no cloud in that part of the sky the luminescence might be part of the sunset.

When they stood still the only sound was the wash of tiny waters under the heather, but even that was less now that the rain was long gone.

'Where did Lyddy go through?' said Keith. 'Just in some random place? Just walked? Nothing in the way?'

'On her quad,' said David. 'Zap, and she wasn't there. And that dog followed her through.'

That dog came panting into the ring of stones, sat Keith down by jumping at his middle, endeavoured to crawl into David's arms, left a wet sign on three stones, and then vanished between two of them, shadow into shadow.

'Like that,' said David. 'This morning. Broad daylight.'

'Just gone home,' said Keith. 'It's not fit to be out. It's not vicious, but it's still not fit, like an act of God.'

'It's gone through,' said David. 'It's in there, yonder.'

'Followed us all the way,' said Keith. 'Then gone past us. Leave it there.'

'Has she come with it?' said David. 'I don't think so. It would have gone back to her.'

'Lyddy,' Keith called. But there was no reply.

'Not here, then,' said David, remembering what had been going on earlier in the day. 'We'd better get the dog back, in case it eats something, bacon sandwich, and so on.'

'Just shout,' said Keith.

'If it's gone through it can't hear us,' said David. 'And it wouldn't come if it did.'

'I knew this would happen,' said Keith, following David, who was following Gytrash. 'You aren't normal.'

Since the spring Nellie Jack John had taken the lamb fences down. The exact trod through was clear.

There was bright daylight, comparatively, beyond the two stones, though dull, with mist floating in the distance like curtains. David looked towards Crackpot Hall, but the mist closed in a furlong. Gytrash was sniffing the ground, trying to find scraps of pop-tart left by Lyddy and Alec-Edward, but having to make do with licking the grass, because this might not be the same morning yonder.

David thrust the last pole into the ground to show which gap was the right way home.

'Eating,' said Keith, as Gytrash licked. 'He won't get back. I mean, if that's the rule that applies.'

'Lyddy brought that through,' said David. 'Except that it isn't there. She was eating here, with a friend.'

Alec-Edward was not here. The little Gytrash was not there. David and Keith were in a cell of mist, with the ground as a floor, and pairs of Jingle Stones making one wall.

'We'll go back,' said Keith. 'Won't we? We can't see into the mist, we don't know when it is or where it is. Or what's here. You keep doing this. It's a defect in your character.'

'Yes,' said David. 'Now I'm doing it on purpose it's a bad habit. But when it was happening to me, when things were talking to me . . .'

'It's a condition,' said Keith. 'You can get stuff for it.'

'When it took over,' said David, 'that was terrifying.'

'I know,' said Keith. 'This could still go wrong. People can't get back in time to rescue us. And this might be the future, not the past.'

Gytrash was now exploring. He did not find it necessary to go back the way he had come, between the same two stones. But when he tried the next space he could not get through. He pawed at the gap, but it was closed against him.

'I think you can't go further on,' said David. 'When we went through in the allotment we just got scared and imagined things. This is somewhere else, but it doesn't mean anything.'

'It means we should go back,' said Keith. 'I don't want to go further on. There might be Attercop. There might be more than one.'

'Lyd and her friend talked about Attercop,' said David. 'It wasn't real that time. My imagination, that's all. You don't need to see Attercop.'

'You certainly don't, said Keith. 'You go back where we came from, the same as we did last time, straight away. Now.'

'But,' said David, 'I'm doing stone circles and monuments. They're my course work speciality. So I can't ignore anything that belongs to them.'

'I can,' said Keith. 'But it's interesting, because if this is another place, who does it belong to? And who can claim it? And how would you sort it out?'

David ignored these legal speculations. Gytrash went through a gap between stones, not the one he had led them through. He came bounding back, with the end of a yell following him, the final part of his own shriek. He counted all his limbs, including his tail, and left a splash against one of the stones.

'That's a message,' said David. 'He can read his own writing. Come on, let's see what he's writing about,' said David. 'We'll go through.'

'Look first,' said Keith. 'Something spooked Gytrash.'

'Let's get spooked too,' said David. 'I'll want a witness, a respectable apprentice solicitor.'

There was the same scenery beyond the gap, inside the circle, but a different night. And perhaps the stones stood tighter, or were more numerous. A bitter wind streaked between them and moaned. There was ice on the ground; there appeared to be ice on the stones, making them bigger, accounting for the crowded effect.

Something moved about in the circle, big, having many legs, seeking a way out, unable to leave.

'Sticky,' said Keith, his hand on the stone beside him. 'Cobweb.'

'It isn't a spider,' said David. 'And it is.'

'Attercop again,' said Keith. 'Get out.'

'It's talking,' said David, because back had come the sense of communication with this other creature, the sense of being told, of being asked. 'Listen.'

Keith was not listening. He was dragging David back. And David, overwhelmed with a huge cloud of otherworld thoughts, dizzy with the blows of information crowding in urgently, allowed himself to be led into daylight, where Gytrash bounded about him.

Keith sat David down. 'I told you,' he said.

'It was too much,' said David. 'If that's Attercop he doesn't want to be here. I think this is all part of the same thing, why there are Jingle Stones, what I was doing in the cave, why I dropped Lyddy at the christening, why I wanted to go through that gap and find Attercop.'

'Let him find his way,' said Keith. He was fumbling in the ground, gathering a handful of water. It's what you give people who have been thrust by shock into collapse and faintness.

'No,' said David. 'This is still the other side. I won't drink it. Even if it was breakfast I wouldn't touch it. You know the rules.'

'Don't drink it, then,' said Keith, and poured it on David's head. 'That's what it's for.'

'God knows,' said David, recovering nicely, 'what you have baptised me into, you great heathen. That might be some infectious religion.'

He was able to stand up, and be led back to midsummer midnight and the Land Rover.

'We'll count them next year,' said Keith. 'This is a leap-midsummer that shouldn't exist.'

SIX

David had thought he would go lamping with Nellie Jack John. Keith thought he might come too, and they were to meet at the bridge over Jingle Beck between the town and Eskeleth.

Twilight was beginning. Already evening rabbits were walking the fields. David came warm to the bridge, where Nellie Jack John sat like a shadow.

David flashed the lamp under the bridge, down the road, into the sky. Sheep gazed back with bored and yellow eyes and went on rasping the grass up.

'Give up, eh,' said Nellie Jack John, because David was stabbing the falling dusk with light.

David switched off the lamp and sat on the bridge parapet, drumming his heels on the stone wall.

'Maybe,' said Nellie Jack John, beginning a sentence and dropping it, knowing what it would say but not how to say it.

'What?' said David, having nothing to say, and wondering how to express that, because it was something and nothing.

Keith came along the road empty-handed. 'I forgot,' he said. 'I forgot.'

'Bang,' said David, in a foolish manner, flashing the lamp at Keith.

'Give up,' said Keith. 'Now I can't see anything.'

'Mebbe we'd best gan home,' said Nellie Jack John. 'There's one of you daft as a brush, and t'other not gitten his gun, so we'd best not start t'job, or we'll kill more than rabbits, and mebbe less.'

'I rang,' said Keith. 'But Eileen said you'd left, John, and there was no reply at David's, only the machine. I forgot my gun was at the shop getting a spring replaced, and I can't bring my dad's out lamping for rabbits.'

'Frank's owd gun is right for t'job,' said Nellie Jack John, 'and one gun isn't plenty.'

David was now standing on the parapet, listening for approaching traffic.

'Eileen's that bothered about the lease and getting turned out in a year or two,' said Keith. 'She just talked about that. I think she thought I was my father, on the telephone.'

Nellie Jack John gazed at the glimmering water below and said nothing, a long sentence of nothing, ignoring David. But he spoke to Keith. 'I can mannish anywhere,' he said. 'Farming and that. I'll frame. But what's to happen to Eileen ails her now.'

Keith nodded. He looked at David. 'Keep still, David,' he said. 'What's the matter with you, too?'

'Daft as a gate,' said Nellie Jack John. 'Too fond to go lamping. I heard him coming three fields off, and he's neither to have nor to hold now he's gitten here.' He had now said his sentence.

David sat down. 'Something coming,' he said. 'Not our car, though.' What he said was full of meaning, but was no explanation.

'Go on,' said Keith. 'What about it not being your car?'

'Oh, it's just them,' said David. 'Gone off on a crusade. It can't be anything, just Lyddy, stirring. Not my fault but she can do no wrong.'

'She stirs,' said Nellie Jack John, sniffing.

Light came leaping among the wayside trees, flooding through the walls and along the road.

Keith was beginning to say that the approaching vehicle was late out on a quiet road, but Nellie Jack John was ahead of him, with a great shout, and standing in the road in the middle of the bridge.

A bus with dark windows stopped, with the engine pattering.

There were shouts back, about having folks in t'beck, thou great fule, and Nellie Jack John telling the driver to mind his job and start frying, very fierce and friendly, and the smell of hot fat walking wide as the bus.

'Three cod,' said Nellie Jack John. 'Chips. Get agait wi't job. Ha' you lads any brass?'

Keith paid. David never had money now, and Nellie Jack John did not carry it except on market days. 'I's never at a shop or owt,' he would say. 'There's nowt to get spent up on in t'fields or on t'moor, but it's easier to come back poorer than richer if you tek brass out and loss it, and if tha goes wi' nowt tha might still find a farthing dropped by some other poor divil.'

Then, 'Vinegar,' he shouted. 'Salt,' and was offered both. All the shouting was a happy joke.

The bus steamed and smoked down the hill, on its way to Gunthwait.

'What like has she done?' Nellie Jack John asked David.

'She cheeked someone,' said David, burning his tongue. 'She wouldn't mean to, it's the way she's brought up.'

'She cheeks everyone,' said Keith. 'So why is this better?'

'She met the divil,' said Nellie Jack John, 'and bested him. Eh?'

'I don't know quite,' said David. 'She got a smack, or something, and they've all got into a state and they've gone to sort it out, see who it was, because Lyddy can't explain, and she doesn't mind, but they're making a fuss.'

'Quite right,' said Keith. 'The rules are different these days.'

But David shook his head. 'They're upset,' he said. 'She isn't. They've gone to look for the house and the woman who slapped her, or whatever it was. So I'm not calm, and they think it was my fault, so I'd be no good lamping and it would be a waste of time anyway. I'll go home and wait for them there.'

'I thought there was summat,' said Nellie Jack John. 'T'rabbits would have gitten the better of thee.'

'It's nothing,' said David. But Nellie Jack John was right, and had been right before David knew.

They were still sitting on the parapet of the bridge when the light from Dr Wix's black Jeep swept down the hill, and Dr Wix was winding down his window.

'Chips, chips, chips,' Lyddy howled over his shoulder, seeing the traces – bags on the bridge, chips going into John's mouth, smelling the floating aura of hot fat and aroma of vinegar.

David handed her the remains of his bag; Nellie Jack John, who had gone on eating, was explaining to her that he had none left; Keith, leaning over to get out of David's way, trod on the fish, slipped, grabbed at David, and pulled both David and himself off the parapet into the beck. Nellie Jack John nodded his head. He had seen it coming.

Lyddy hung over the parapet to shout and encourage. 'He didn't do it,' she called and called. No one knew which side she was on, and they were both insisting that he did.

'I saw him,' Lyddy yelled. 'I saw him.'

'I'm going home,' Dr Wix told them after a time. 'No, Lyddy, I've not going to drop you in after them.'

'But I daren't jump,' said Lyddy. 'So how will I get down there.'

'Going home,' said Dr Wix. 'If you want a ride.'

David went with him, in his underwear. Nellie Jack John strode up the hill to Swang Farm. Keith went with David, walking at first to get dry for the car, unable to let Lyddy see him at all unclothed.

'But I want to see your bobo,' she told him.

'That's a matter of client confidentiality,' said Keith. She thought that could be cured, and ought to have been.

'I blame the father,' said Dr Wix, at last.

'He hasn't got one,' said Lyddy, dissolving into extreme mirth and hiccups. No one asked her what she meant.

It wasn't all that funny, David thought. She made that up. She's hiding something.

She thought she had hidden it. She had been out with both parents to find the house where the lady had hit her with a stick, scolded her and told her she was an ill-mannered child.

'It wasn't me,' she told David.

But Dr Wix and Kirstie had taken her to the house. Lyddy knew exactly where it was. She had walked there, she said, but knew the car way even better.

'We'll just tell the stick lady to keep her stick to herself,' Dr Wix said, meaning that there would be a row. 'I'm not sure which house you mean, Lyddy.'

In broad daylight, and going by car, Lyddy could not find it either. 'You cross the beck here,' she said. 'She'll hit you.'

They crossed the beck there.

'What house?' Dr Wix had asked, looking through a gateway at a field.

'It was the other day,' said Lyddy. 'Alec-Edward . . .' But so far she had not explained Alec-Edward at home, and said no more now.

'I don't know them these days,' said Dr Wix.

Kirstie had got out of the Jeep and gone through the gate. There was no house. There was a wall marking an oblong. There was a row of trees that had once been a hedge. There was a flagged floor standing in the grass unfurnished, no longer a room. There was one fireplace standing in a stump of wall.

Lyddy was realising she had said more than she meant, given away her trips beyond the Jingle Stones to other times and other people, and would be the one in trouble. Though Kirstie said, 'Poor pet,' Lyddy could not explain.

'Eskeleth Hall,' said Dr Wix, later on at home, looking on the maps. 'Site of Eskeleth Hall.'

'Demolished in 1832,' Kirstie read in a local history book.

'Lots of other people,' said Lyddy. She had been thinking, and happily about truth. Not the relevant truth, but a provident one. 'It was one of them. It was in a picture at school, Mrs Strong showed us. She said they had history then, and if you didn't curtsey you got whipped.'

'Well, you've got a bump of direction,' said Kirstie, 'to find the place like that from a picture.'

'It doesn't hurt any more,' said Lyddy, patting her bottom kindly. 'Jackie Thornborrow taught me how to curtsey, but you don't have to fall over like she did.'

SEVEN

Ten days later Keith summoned David to Swang Farm for a conference.

'Right,' said David, without having any need for more explanation. Keith had clearly spoken to his father.

At Swang Eileen and Frank were waiting by the kitchen fire. Keith had driven the office car up from the office in town, bringing with him a briefcase containing papers and a lap-top.

David had driven the Land Rover down from Crackpot Hall. Nellie Jack John said milking could wait a lile bit, and scrubbed his hands clean at the kitchen sink, whilst Eileen pushed him about, trying to get to the sink herself to fill the kettle. For her no conference was valid without a pot of tea.

'And parkin,' she said, filling a plate with it.

Nellie Jack John put a piece in his mouth. 'I's glad to hear summat,' he said through it. 'By rights it should be my lease at Swang, when all's said.'

Keith was to say it. He had papers to prove it.

'The trust was set up in about 1750,' he said. 'To run two hundred and fifty years or so. Then it runs out and has to be renewed. It must have seemed so far ahead that it couldn't matter.'

'Plenty of folk get a lease renewed,' said Frank. 'And it's always been a market rent.'

'We've seen to that,' said Keith. 'My father thinks that the firm before Heseltines set the trust up in the 1750s, and Heseltines took over a hundred years later, in the time of my great-great-grandfather. But there's only one document left, an indenture on parchment. We haven't got it in the office, but we're looking for it.'

'We've paid our rent,' said Frank. 'My Dad before me, and his before him, and it's like it was our place all the way through.'

'Never missed,' said Eileen. 'Except once when Frank and your father were both bad and couldn't meet or get to the post-box.'

'It's nothing to do with that,' said Keith. 'Neither of you need think about it.' But Eileen still looked worried, and old, and withdrawn; and, worst of all, thin.

'It's an old house, and the land has probably been farmed for several thousand years,' said Keith. 'There have been times when there wasn't a tenant, and it's been empty. The new lease began after one of those times, or when it changed owners.'

David was wondering about the possibility of some quick joke to cheer Eileen up. He was checking whether it would be possible to make Frank smile, when he caught Frank's eyes, and saw a smile in them, and understood that the joke was already happening, about Keith, and the way he was taking charge of the conference, knew what he was talking about, and was going to deal with matters as well as they could be dealt with. He even had his little briefcase leaning against his chair, and any moment now might bring out the lap-top and pluck information out of the air. But Keith saw how Frank was eyeing him, and left the computer where it was.

David said nothing. The chairman of the meeting was still totally Keith, but Keith with something more added, Keith as he always had been, but with all the elements working together and making something else. This was Keith in spite of Dr Tate, in spite of knowing David all his life, unharmed by existence so far, not a hunk, but a Fonz.

So that was good. But it was bad too, because Keith had become by now everything he could be, David thought; everything that was in him was in full use, and there were no more resources. All his wit and wisdom and jokes were already fully deployed, and he could now be relied on to do everything right, and generally be trusted not to think otherwise.

David nodded to Frank, to show he understood; Eileen looked unhappy at what she was being told.

'We,' Keith was saying, 'my father and I, the firm, Heseltines, who are the trustees set up by the owner, are unable to offer a further lease because we no longer know who the owners are, because they have dropped out of sight.'

'They'll have a name,' said Frank. 'They'll be called summat, Mister, Sir, Lord, Lady. There'll be a signature somewhere. Esquire, or the like. There's awlus grand folk wi' a stick to mense bairns' manners.'

'They haven't a name we can read,' said Keith, 'They never had a signature. They called themselves Swang Farm. In those days, if you couldn't write you signed with a seal. That doesn't always say the name, but people knew you by your sign, your seal.'

David watched Eileen. She is going to say 'Flipper', he decided. Eileen certainly had a struggle, but what she said was, 'Wax?' and pressed her thumb on the table.

'The owner's sign,' said Keith. He looked at the table, while he felt in his pocket for something. 'The deed has been with the Land Registry for thirty years at least, ever since the Registry was set up, in my grandfather's time. They're trying to find it. I can't help you.' He did not find anything in his pocket except dust, which he dropped on the fire.

'We've paid rent for long enough,' said Frank. 'Ninety year and more, I heard my grandad say sitting in this very chair by this selfsame fireplace; ninety years of rents, four times a year.'

'Eating the same parkin,' said Eileen.

'I doubt,' said Frank. 'He'd lossed his teeth by I knew him, but not his senses, and he was talking of his father, way back.'

'It's a pity,' said Keith. 'But with not knowing who the owner is, and very likely no argument about it, you could have given up paying rent seventy years ago, and after a few years claimed the property as your own. But we couldn't advise that, acting for them.'

'I could always do without paying the rent,' said Frank. 'But I would miss it. Owing the rent always sharpened up my work, and paying it kept me in with a solicitor if I ever needed one.'

'That's right,' said Eileen. 'Well, Keith, you haven't told us much.'

'And now's the time I need a solicitor,' said Frank. 'So what now?'

'When the lease ends,' said Keith, 'you'll be able to get a new lease from a new owner, but maybe only a short one, and on new terms.'

'Born here,' said Frank. 'I'll die here, me and Eileen.'

'Oh Frank,' said Eileen, 'not yet, lad.'

'And t'bloody boggarts,' said Frank. 'Maybe. But what about Nellie Jack John, here? What's for our lad, eh?'

'We'll do our best,' said Keith, gathering up papers and taking up his briefcase. 'Without instructions from the owner we can't get any further.'

'We know you'll do best for us,' said Frank. 'We've known you this long time.' He looked to Eileen and David to confirm what he said.

'And,' said Nellie Jack John, 'I've kenned thee lang eneugh, sithee.'

Eileen got behind these kind remarks with her own bleak worry. She said, 'But now there's nowt you can do, is that it?'

'Without the owner's permission, not much, Eileen,' said Keith. 'And who's to pay us if we go to the courts to sort it out? Judges cost more than you'll want to pay, and we advise against trying; and the owners, who are a sort of company called Swang Farm, can't be made to pay. So we've to see what turns up. Maybe the owners will declare themselves. And there isn't just the property to deal with, but a few other things too.'

Which must be true, coming from this new and competent lawyer.

He left then, looking at his watch, ready for some other appointment. Frank and Eileen sat and looked at the fire.

'My grandad never had this worry,' said Frank. 'Teeth or not, fire or not.'

'I'll get milking,' said Nellie Jack John. 'You stop in the warm.' He nodded his head to David, who was not sure whether to go or stay, but Nellie Jack John knew he should go, and he left just after Keith.

'What can I say?' said Keith. 'We have to abide by the agreements. We're getting the indenture from the Registry, but we've never seen it ourselves. We only had the seal, because the ribbon broke and it was in the box. I meant to bring it, but it must be in my other jacket. It doesn't mean anything, just a design of a cup. My father says big estates had a rent cup for the tenants to put their rent in to make it legal, and the picture on the seal would remind them.'

'What can we do?' said David. 'They're miserable.'

'Stick to the rules,' said Keith.

EIGHT

Kirstie thought that Lyddy must be drinking it, she said. 'It doesn't have any effect on her hair,' she said, giving David the name of shampoo, if he happened to be going past the chemist in town. 'And now there isn't any in the house.'

'My hair is so constipated,' said Lyddy.

David followed Dr Tate into the shop the next day, and that was mere chance. Dr Tate was searching his wallet for the ticket for his photographs and not looking where his feet went.

That he trod on the person called Metcalfe, who was an assistant and flat on the floor looking under a stand for some lost article, was mere accident.

'Theophany?' he asked her, remembering when she had lain on the grass and listened at the centre of the Jingle Stones. He had tiresome habits of recall.

'Individual bath salts,' she said. 'Gorrunder. Oh yeah, I remember, up at them spooky stones.'

'I remember too,' said Dr Tate. 'If you'll stand aside I'll continue with my business. After all, it's bad luck to walk over a fallen Metcalfe.'

'It's bloody bad luck to be one,' she said, scrambling up. 'It's kessoned, anyroad,' and she handed him a lilac cube with a torn cellophane wrapping and a bent corner.

David, passing by on the other side of the stockade of goods, heard the section of meaningless dialogue, and understood it. He sorted his way through the shampoo, and began to make his way to the check-out, through all the scents and glitter of the shop. Dr Tate was at the photography counter, misunderstanding another ex-pupil who was on duty there. Fluorescent lamps flickered and buzzed, and David thought of the subterranean voice of God.

Something was happening to him. The fragment of speech between Metcalfe and Tate, he thought, had woken something up. What was around him gathered into a further meaning. He held on to the display, beyond the shampoos, where it began to be baby stuff, and stood as if contemplating a purchase. He had often bought nappies here for Lyddy.

Feeding cup, he said to himself, reading the objects in front of him. Tubs of cotton buds. A solid plastic bib with a rim to catch overflowing food. A graduated feeding bottle (Dr Tate, David thought, Dr of Philosophy, feeding kids knowledge).

Just a sense, he told himself, that things have a meaning, when they don't. They want to be seen through, and show something beyond.

All they showed and had in common was the reflection of overhead striplights, swaying under his gaze; all reflection, not the things themselves, light like candle flames. and beyond that light something the far side of theophany, the voice that is not a voice, the wings falling.

Time's tunnel forming between those fallen wings and the ground; ground so cold, where there should be no ground; being able to see into that ground.

Not me, not myself, David was struggling to understand. Words kept getting in his way. He was trying to reach something that did not use words; something was trying to reach him through direct and shared experience, not through ears, sounds, meanings.

The experience could not be shared, because the thing connecting to him could not explain what it saw, what it conveyed to him as if they were each a broken kind of the other.

The cold ground, translucent. Ice, David thought. I have seen ice. But this much ice is geological, which I have not seen.

Vivid wings overhead were detached, spinning, floating, drifting away, gone and broken, fading like a dream, and a thing did not need explaining, the longing, being lost far from family or . . .

'More theophany, Wix?' said Dr Tate, swinging by in his own thoughts.

'It's the lights,' said David, confused by the brilliance, baffled by the thoughts or senses now simmering in a corner of his mind, an alien program running on his private screen.

'Are you well?' asked Dr Tate. He was a doctor of philosophy, so it was no good having physical symptoms. David gaped at him, and felt foolish.

'Come outside,' said Dr Tate, a hand ready to catch David if he swooned.

Outside, David got over the gape and said, 'I'm all right,' because he was, apart from the presence of another mind within his; and a strong sense of having been forced through the mind of a spider. 'It's all nonsense. I haven't paid for the shampoo.'

'I'll get the person called Metcalfe,' said Dr Tate. 'She can sort it out.'

'Yeah,' she said, coming out, going in and transacting, coming out again. 'No problem. There you go.'

'Can I leave you?' asked Dr Tate, leaving without a reply. 'You'll be all right, I'm sure, with Metcalfe.' He handed David the crumbled bath cube with thoughtful disdain, and left the scene.

Another scene stayed with David, but not a scene of the visible. It ran in his mind like a fragment of dream, playing its sorrow, displaying its loss.

It's there, David thought. It is trying to make its history my history, if I will share it. I have only to listen.

But listening was not the simple act needed. David knew that. He no longer listened, or saw, but knew.

He knew where the ice was. He knew what was under the ice. He knew why the ice was still there, and not there too. He knew about theophany and where it was, and why. Something had aligned itself with his mind. For moments, in the market place, against the modern vertical ice of the plate glass window, David feared that it was madness. But it was clearly outside himself, not seeking a way in, only giving a message.

The message was without words, without feelings, without

emotion towards David. It was clear though it was surrounded by fear, terror, and desolation. And while some of it was outside understanding, the reasons, or causes, were clear.

'Attercop,' said David, constructing in his mind but knowing he was still being inexact. 'I know, I know. It has been telling me for years. And everything else begins to mean something.' He saw round him, here and now, then and there, the church in the market place, the castle keep beyond, the ice-cream stall, the Land Rover standing rough among the sweet saloons. He held the bottle of shampoo and knew what it was.

'They sent me to ask you,' said the person called Metcalfe, Sally, 'are you right? I wouldn't ask with Tate joining in.'

'Yes,' said David. 'Thank you very much, Sally,' he went on, meaning it completely, because the theophany had been hers and he had had to know about it; but could not explain because all the facts that could be useful for that, or useful for anything, were still lying disconnected in his mind.

'Just asking,' she said. 'That's all.'

'Fine,' said David. 'Just stuff in my head.'

Towards eight o'clock he walked to the hillside above Swang Farm, because this was where he might encounter the other reality, and begin to meet its needs.

NINE

David was not the first at the Jingle Stones. Before he reached them there was a car in the yard at Swang, and moments later a solitary figure began to walk up the hill towards the moor.

David saw the walker turn into Keith. David walked away from the stones and between the rounded heaps that made the moor like a rough cloth over a tray of rising bread rolls.

He won't notice me even if I wave and shout, thought David. I'll just sit here. What does he want?

Keith paused at the top gate to catch his breath. David would not have let him, if they had been together. But Keith was on his own. David sat against the poised and bare stones of a pitch of scree and watched.

Keith came on, watching the ground, not looking to either side. He rested again when he reached the stones. He walked round outside, then went in, cautiously. He was too busy with his own intentions to keep any sort of watch. David moved up on him, and stood behind one of the stones.

Keith has heard the same things, he said to himself. Attercop. It is coming together for us. Maybe he knows more than I do. I am not ready to explain anything.

Keith chalked on some of the stones with the chalk from the game of rock chess. David decided he ought not to spy on Keith, and went to join him. But when he came into the ring of stones it was empty. Where Keith had gone he could not tell, because there were marks and numbers on several stones. The methods were no doubt precise but entirely Keith's own. What they were for was not clear. David shouted three times, and there was no reply.

David did what he had come to do. The person called Metcalfe had lain on the moist grass. He knelt in that place, with his hands on small boulders that filled the space.

He thought he felt a thrill through the stone, but could not be sure. He had to lie down, as Sally had lain down. He put his ear against the ground.

There was theophany. The ground shook with it, without quite moving his head. With his teeth slack against each other he felt them sing. With his fingertips poised on a low rock he let them tingle.

Something wanted to share thoughts with him. Perhaps it was sharing them with Keith as well and had drawn him through to the other side. They were here independently, and Keith had come here on his own business, in his own time, and alone. He might not want to share his journey or his thoughts.

But there's a common cause, David decided. Keith can't have any other ideas except the one that has come to me. That's the logic of it.

Meanwhile another clamour of thought from elsewhere

came to him. I am sane, David thought. Apart from lying in a wet patch being looked at by a fattish but uneasy lamb. Long ago these thoughts came on me all at once, when they were welcome and happy, when I could not make any analysis, and did not know what anything meant. I had no information, only vast quantities of sensation, and did not know how to act.

He did not know how to act now, only that there was some need for him to do so. Keith should have waited, he thought. We should have done it together. I should have come to meet him. Why didn't I?

But what for? It was still not clear. There were certainties, connected with the stones, and with the cave where he had been found by Keith, and a conviction that the centre of the circle, where theophany rang, and the cave were the same place, the centre of the circle the epicentre of the cave down below.

Someone was shouting. David sat up and stood up. There was a thrill of small hooves. Sheep were being moved past the Jingle Stones, bleating and bawling.

'Now then,' called Nellie Jack John. Jip came to herd David in with the flock, until John catapulted some words and whistles to him.

'Lamb sales,' John called, and went on his way down the hill towards Swang Farm.

Keith was there, standing and watching the sheep.

'Couldn't you get through?' he asked.

'I hadn't tried,' said David. 'I thought it just happened, if it did.'

'You go across the middle first,' said Keith. 'Nellie Jack John told me.'

'And then where?' said David. 'The cave?'

'Maybe,' said Keith. The idea seemed new to him. 'Happen,' he said, in the local dialect.

'Where, Clementine?' said David, insulting his friend. 'Why?'

'Down into town,' said Keith.

'You have clients there?' asked David.

'The Jurassic bank robbery,' said Keith. 'The Dinosaur divorce case. You know. Confidential.'

'Yes,' said David. 'The Pterodactyl Playground Persecution Prosecution.'

'In that,' said Keith, solemnly, 'we're acting for the other side.'

TEN

At the end of the day Lyddy would speak to no one, except to tell them so. Otherwise she screamed, so loudly that all the jackdaws flew away. She broke her boycott of everyone else to say that even her tame one had gone, and she didn't know which it was, and both matters were family faults she greatly deprecated, so there.

'No, no, no,' said Kirstie. 'Once and for all and for ever, no. And that pork pie was our supper.'

That day Kirstie had been doing accounts, which accounted for the pork pie and no cooking. Lyddy had come out from school, observed by David and Keith from the top of the track, started the quad, and come home. Gytrash went to meet her, and stood up on the machine behind her, driving just as well as Lyddy.

'After that I thought she was with you,' Kirstie said to David. 'Our systems aren't perfect. I hope the crows come back. But I have to finish the bills, so you're in charge of her screaming her head off.'

There was nothing to do. Lyddy sat on the stairs and drummed her heels. Kirstie said, 'Fifty-eight fifty, arrow arrow bank account 'b', credit, that's the pink column, command, right arrow, check column, go back to interest, fifty-eight fifty.' She had been doing this stuff all the afternoon. 'It doesn't get any better.'

Lyddy had been doing something different. She had put the quad in its shed, come in, found several biscuits, put some into her mouth and some into her pocket, some into Gytrash, and had more in her hand for when there was room in her mouth, and gone outside.

David and Keith had seen all these actions, and mentioned them to Lyddy. She had merely given them an evil look, spluttered out a few crumbs that silenced them, and continued going outside.

She had been on the swing for a time, because everybody heard the restless wheezing of its chains. Then there had been quiet, except for the buzzing of Kirstie's printer. Lyddy and Gytrash were not making a noise.

David made coffee in a peaceful kitchen. Keith swept up biscuit crumbs. The biscuits themselves had gone.

An hour later Lyddy was banging open the bottom half of the kitchen door and coming in.

'Don't go out again, Lyddy,' Kirstie called. 'Daddy will be back soon.'

'We won't,' Lyddy called.

'No dogs in the house,' Kirstie called back, almost getting up to see about it, but being held back by some complicated amount she was sorting into the spreadsheet.

'No,' Lyddy called back, banging shut the door between kitchen and house in a rather suspect way.

'If he's in, he's in,' said Kirstie, thinking about Gytrash. 'David, come and sort out this formula for me, I've damaged it.'

That took some time. By the time it was done Dr Wix was home and had come into the house through the kitchen.

'I'll stop and get something to eat,' said Kirstie.

'No hurry,' said Dr Wix. 'I'll just run this child home first. I haven't the faintest idea who he is.'

Lyddy was ready to explain. 'It's Alec-Edward,' she said. 'It was raining where he lives, so he lives here now. You'll have to get him a quad, but he can share Gytrash and my room.'

Alec-Edward was at the kitchen table, looking at an empty plate.

'So we don't need any supper,' said Lyddy, picking a strand of pork pie jelly from the plate, dangling it from her fingers, and licking it into her mouth.

'But that's our pork pie,' said Kirstie.

Alec-Edward belched like a cow. He was looking very solemn.

'But that's Alec-Edward,' said David, coming into the room.

'Then you know where he lives, David,' said Dr Wix. 'Can you take him home?'

For the time being all this was nothing to Keith. Lyddy had her friends, and that was all he knew, or needed to know. He left the family to sort out their muddle, and waited outside for the right moment to say goodbye. That moment was near, because Kirstie was becoming angry.

'Take him home?' said David. 'I don't know. What's he been doing?'

'Getting his tea,' said Lyddy.

'All of it,' said Kirstie. 'Between them they've eaten the whole of the pork pie.'

'Breacus,' said David, reminded of what Nellie Jack John had said about eating the wrong side of your reality.

'Tea,' said Alec-Edward. 'It were grand.'

Keith came back into the kitchen when he heard the word 'Breacus'. 'What do you mean?' he asked.

'It means there's no supper,' said Kirstie.

'There's pickled onions,' said Lyddy. 'Two.'

'I'll try to sort this out,' said David. 'Lyddy, Alec-Edward, go and get in my Land Rover.'

'But it's too late,' said Keith. 'If, you know, what you said.'

'That child's eaten too much,' said Dr Wix.

'I had some of it,' said Lyddy.

'I can tell,' said Keith. 'I'm the signs of cream officer.'

Lyddy licked her guilty lips.

Alec-Edward belched again, turned pale, and swallowed desperately. His eyes grew round. He held on to his overdose of pork pie, but only just.

'Bucket,' said Dr Wix, pitching a mop out of one and handing the useful receptacle to David.

'Of course,' said David, holding it towards Alec-Edward. 'But I'm used to Keith's jokes because he never makes them.'

'I don't understand,' said Kirstie. 'But he's not staying, so I don't care what you do, so long as you get him out of my kitchen. Lyddy doesn't know what she's doing.'

'We'll do our best,' said David. 'She's kidnapped him, and he shouldn't be here.'

'But he likes it here,' said Lyddy, 'so I do know what I am doing.' She certainly understood what she meant.

'He's the only one,' said Kirstie. 'As you'll soon find out, my lass.'

David was hustling Alec-Edward off his chair and out of the room.

'Thirty years ago,' said Dr Wix, 'some families smelt; but not these days, surely, and never quite like that. So who is he?'

Gytrash licked Alec-Edward's face. Alec-Edward had nothing to say. Lyddy pulled at one arm, to get him back in the house, David held the other and took him to the Land Rover.

'Bring the bucket,' he told Keith.

'I'll just go home,' said Keith. 'This isn't the perfect end to a summer's day.'

'Come on,' said David. 'Just hold it. He's going to need it, and if he doesn't I don't know what happens. I don't want pork-pie sick all over the Landy.'

Keith was thinking that since the Land Rover was not his he did not care. But he got into the back, with Alec-Edward beside him, and held the bucket.

'You've got to show us the way,' David told Lyddy. 'Did you get him from the Jingle Stones?'

'I'm going to stay here,' said Lyddy. 'And make Alec-Edward's bed. They don't want him at the Jingle Stones.'

David picked her up and thrust her into the back of the Land Rover. Gytrash leapt in after her. David drove into the

131

long lane that led along the hill towards Swang and the Jingle Stones.

Alec-Edward went to sleep. Keith bit his tongue when the Land Rover hit the dry ruts. Lyddy was talking, but no one could hear her. Gytrash looked over the driver's shoulder, barking in David's ear to point out interesting features in the landscape. Alec-Edward woke up, looked at the bucket, but held on to his tea, and closed his eyes.

When the car stopped by the stones Lyddy was reaching the end of her speech. If Alec-Edward was going back, she said, she was going with him. Not at once, she stated, but when she had been home and got the quad and all her gear. 'I'll need a trailer,' she said.

'No problem,' said David, pulling her out of the way and dragging Alec-Edward out after her, holding him to one side, in case.

'He wasn't,' said Keith. 'He fell asleep.'

'It's the only thing I can think of,' said David. 'Or he's here for ever.'

Alec-Edward was sleepy and miserable. Lyddy was resigned to what was happening.

'I'll get him again tomorrow,' she said. 'One day.'

'Show us the way,' said David. 'Hurry up.'

'No,' said Lyddy, pacing about to find the centre of the Jingle Stones. 'This is the way.' She began to walk slowly to the gap between two stones. 'It was this afternoon.'

It was the way. She grew hazy as she walked, and disappeared when she reached the stones. She was back in sight in a moment, crawling on all fours. 'I went too fast,' she wailed, and began to make ugly noises she could not help.

Keith looked away. Lyddy being sick over there was better than expecting someone else to be sick in the bucket he was holding. It was also useless, he thought. Alec-Edward was the one who had eaten the wrong side and who had to have that eating cancelled.

'Wrong one,' said David. 'Make him sick, Keith.'

Lyddy snivelled. Alec-Edward began to whimper. He called for his Mam, turned round towards Keith, and was sick over Keith's shoes, once, twice, three times; then a rest, and three more heaves, and there was nothing left.

'Hell,' said Keith, and went off to find a gutter to rinse his feet in.

'I had a puke,' said Alec-Edward, spitting out fragments. 'By God.' He felt well again. 'What are we off to do?'

'Go home,' said David. 'They're laiting of you.'

Alec-Edward went through to his own side a moment later. Lyddy washed his face for him with her sleeve, and came back to her own side of the stones.

'Tomorrow,' she said, climbing soberly into the Land Rover, determined to have her own way.

'You smell awful,' said David.

Keith smelt worse when he came back from the water. He would not be without his trousers with Lyddy there.

Gytrash smelt worst. He had been eating recent delicacies among the stones, and had to walk home on his own. He had rolled in some choice bits.

Lyddy had her story ready for Kirstie. 'I was sick,' she said. No one could be angry with a person who had been sick, could they?

'It makes no difference,' said Kirstie. 'You can remember that, and you can remember not to bring people home with you and feed them all our supper. That was enough pork pie for five people.'

'Four people,' said Lyddy, to make things better. 'I don't like pork pie any more.' But nothing was made better, because pertness was being added to thoughtlessness.

David took Keith a pair of trousers, socks, and shoes, outside. Inside Kirstie reduced Lyddy to silence, then to defiance, screaming, and stamping. Dr Wix walked round the garden.

'Worse than you,' he told David. 'Some act. What's she going to be like?'

'She's actually like a boggart already,' said David.

In the old stable Gytrash was howling, and chewing the door, kicking it like a horse.

Lyddy was getting into the last attitudes of the day, and going to bed, she said. 'Just go,' said Kirstie. 'I won't help you; I have plenty to do already. If you want to scream about that you're welcome. We all have better to do than help you by listening.'

Lyddy was not out of options yet. 'Keith can put me to bed,' she said. 'He is the best at stories.'

'I am not,' said Keith. 'I can only do evidence.' But he went upstairs. He was down immediately, followed by shouts from Lyddy.

'She's taken all her clothes off,' he said, insulted by such carelessness. 'And got in the bath, and splashed me when I wasn't ready. And she's got black patches all over her.'

'That's how it's done, Keith,' said Kirstie. 'When she comes out just dry her, tell her a story, and if you make it dull enough she'll be asleep by the time you finish. The black patches are ink; they've been making it at school. Nellie Jack John took them the stuff.'

'Her breath smells,' said Keith. 'Of sick.'

'You're going to get her to clean her teeth,' said Kirstie.

'All those things,' said Dr Wix.

'Say her prayers,' said David. 'Listen up and tell us who she prays to.'

From his room David heard the story beginning.

'This indenture witnesseth,' said Keith, 'dated once upon a time, the agreement between the mother of the first part, Little Red Riding Hood of the second part, and the grandmother of the third part, the big bad wolf intervening; who have set their signatures and seals to this indenture –'

'Gytrash,' said Lyddy, face down, one eye showing, backside a mountain on the bed.

'– forasmuch as,' said Keith, 'the party of the first part and the party of the second part have entered into a settled determination that the party of the second part shall take such goods and chattels as provided willingly and in good faith by the party of the first part to the party—'

'You can't come to it,' said Lyddy, the solitary eye fluttering. 'It's only boys.'

'—of the third part and shall pursue a course along the little path through the forest deviating neither from the right side nor the left of the right of way granted by custom time out of mind, since Sunday, eleventh of December, 1154; furthermore that the said goods and chattels comprising a bottle of dandelion and burdock—'

'Bowk,' said the mountain.

'—a margherita pizza, a tin of baked beans, a bunch of flowers, to wit, I mean to wilt, bluebells and wild roses, shall be delivered intact to the party of the third part; and in respect to the law of the realm of fancy the big bad wolf shall intervene at point A on the plan hereto attached and marked with a red bloodstain and shall lawfully and with malignant intent demand of the party of the second part what is in her basket and the party of the second part shall dutifully reply, Goods and chattels comprising a bottle of dandelion and burdock, a margherita pizza, a tin of baked beans, a bunch of flowers, to wit and to wilt from this day forth, bluebells and wild roses, to be delivered intact to the party of the third part in accordance with the agreement entered into between the party of the second part and the party of the first part notwithstanding the intervention of the intervenor the big bad wolf.'

'Keith,' said Lyddy, with her sweet dentifrice breath, eyes closed, subsiding.

'Yes,' said Keith.

'Shut up,' said Lyddy. 'I'm tired.'

She was nicer when she could only say 'Eef,' thought Keith. And couldn't walk.

ELEVEN

Nellie Jack John was sitting alone in a field above Swang, doing nothing, apparently, with a big old-fashioned cloth sack beside him. The tractor was at the bottom of the field. The dog Jip was not there.

Nellie Jack John turned his head slowly to look at David and Keith. His skin was the colour of cloud, white, grey, and bruised on its own without having been hit. His eyes were yellow, his lips black.

'He's dead,' said Keith, convinced it was so, that dead bodies turned their heads and watched blankly as you approached.

'I isn't,' said Nellie Jack John, in a voice very like a corpse. 'I've tewed myself dragging this sack. Give us a hand to t'tractor, and I's right.'

'You don't look right,' said David.

'I've gitten teng'd by summat,' said Nellie Jack John. Teng'd meant bitten or stung.

A smell of great foulness came from the sack, combining a septic midden and a dead rat, with overtones of rain beetle and burying beetle. It made David's throat contract and his stomach rebel. He was able to speak, but took care not to get the noxious vapour into his mouth.

'What is it?' he asked.

'Dead yowe, happen,' said Nellie Jack John.

David said nothing. It must be Jip in the sack, he thought, found dead and rotting, a farm dog valued almost more than any other thing or person, and the matter with Nellie Jack John be grief at the loss of a friend and a value.

Keith covered his mouth and nose with his shirt.

'Get it to t'tractor,' said Nellie Jack John. 'Put it in t'box. Come back for me. I isn't right good.'

The sack was full, but not so heavy as David expected. The mouth of it had been tied with baler twine, and there were long ends that were merely tarry, not stinking. At the tractor they had to hold the other corners to heave the sack into the box.

'Feels like twigs,' said David. 'What's he going to do with it? Bury it?'

Nellie Jack John was not answering questions. They stood him up, and he asked for air, and bent double with agony to draw it in.

He's going to be sick on my feet, thought Keith. But Nellie Jack John swallowed that impulse back, and managed to walk. His left arm and left leg, and all that side of him, were tettered with spasms of agony; that hand was swollen and blotched yellow and purple; his left leg had swollen and distended his knee to fill his jeans, and almost could not be bent.

'We'd better put you in the box and drive you on down,' said David.

'I'll frame,' said Nellie Jack John. 'I've that much to do I can't stop to die, sithee.'

They had to heave him up into the tractor cab. He leaned on the wheel and looked at the sky. Then he started the engine, leaned on the clutch with his whole body, and got into gear and away. They watched him down the fields and into the yard at Swang. They saw him get down and drag the sack into a shed at the end of the buildings, where Frank Watson used to boil pig feed in the set-pot, or copper.

Nellie Jack John came out, hobbled across the yard, and let himself into the house.

'Eileen won't care for that stink,' said Keith.

'It must have been Jip,' said David.

'No,' said Keith.

At that moment Jip came through the top gate, following a scent without getting close to it, growling at it, not wanting to approach it.

'I could follow it,' said David. 'It's that strong.'

'It could follow me,' said Keith.

Jip glanced at them, swung his tail, and went down the field, now and then snarling at the trail, the smell.

'A boggart?' David said.

'We ought to go and check on him,' said Keith. 'Nellie Jack John, not the boggart.'

'He'll know what teng'd him,' said David, 'and the cure.'

'There isn't a cure,' said Keith. 'He's been stung by Attercop. Attercop has been killing sheep.'

David's mind wiped itself empty, and then came back on the

screen of consciousness. It was more or less the same, but there was an extra menu in his awareness, and the cursor of his mind about to pull it down.

'I'd forgotten,' he said. 'There used to be something in my memory. I used to think it was madness, but it wasn't in charge, so I stopped worrying. Then it went away.'

'It can stay away,' said Keith. 'Can't it? That's in your mind, but if Attercop's about then he might attack Lyddy. Even Jip is afraid of him.'

'Attercop is dead,' said David. 'It was in the sack, Keith. Nothing else smells like Attercop.'

'Who says there's only one?' said Keith, putting forward an idea, rather than saying what he had once seen.

'Who says there's any?' said David. 'It was a dead yowe, rotting meat, rotting wool, all turned to smelly fat in a bog hole full of water; that was the smell, like pus gone bad.'

Keith wanted that to be so, an explainable smell; for Nellie Jack John's bite to be from venomous moorland snake, a hagworm; no Attercop; no inexplicable thoughts in David's head.

'Waxy and rancid,' said David. 'There's a name for it.'

'I don't want to know it,' said Keith. 'Let's go back to yesterday, or last week, or anywhere, and turn left at the interchange, because this road is rubbish.'

That made good sense, because they were on the way to collect David's Land Rover, down in the town for a new fuel tank, and the way there was along the lane. They got back to that and walked on.

The reek of dead creature began to leave them. A runnel of water crossed the lane, and they ran their hands through it and used mud as a soap to pull the smell from their skin.

'We'll come back by Swang,' said David. 'See how he is.'

'Cramp, or something,' said Keith.

'I don't know,' said David. 'Remember when Lyddy was a baby, and we both got remembering about when I got lost? Well, there were other things, like a story about another world, that kept coming to my mind.'

'You said a bit about it,' said Keith. 'Then you stopped saying it. It was a sort of fancy.'

'It was real,' said David. He had pulled down the menu in his mind, and found things listed in a sensible way. 'It's taken a long time to sort out. They should have chosen someone older in the first place. I've only just got round to understanding it.'

Keith had not got so far. He said so. 'I don't know what it is at all,' he said.

'It's time,' said David. 'Something that happened a long time . . . not ago, but away. I think it's the future.'

'It will be,' said Keith.

'How do you know?' said David.

'Joke,' said Keith. 'The future will be; it hasn't already been.'

'Keith,' said David, 'shut up. Your jokes are not quite funny. They're not even better than nothing. The future. Explaining Attercop, and everything, Alec-Edward, Nellie Jack John, and other things I don't know about. I was told about it. There's information in my mind. Something in the future came back here. It's when humans are extinct.'

141

'All of us?' said Keith.

'One by one,' said David. Dr Tate had talked about the extinction of species, cheerfully concluding that no one felt lonely because a sudden earthquake killed the lot off at once, and there was no last monarch of consciousness mourning the demise of his kind. The person called Metcalfe had said it would be a pity about the shops, eh; Dr Tate had grumbled that some people were already extinct but hadn't the grace to admit it, Metcalfe.

'So who came back?' said Keith, answering David, in the long lane millennia before extinction, years after Dr Tate's speech.

'An arthropod,' said David. 'Like spiders. I kept hearing about webs, feeling them, getting them in my mouth. In the future somebody, one of them, had to come back and tell me about it. I expect ordinary spiders say it quite a lot but we can't hear it. So you know about it too. They made an element . . .'

'Made an element?' said Keith. 'You can't make elements; they just come naturally.'

'We're extinct,' said David. 'Earthquake. Spideries have taken over.'

'Makes sense,' said Keith. If you happen to be mad, his eyes indicated.

'The fools,' said David. 'Inheriting consciousness and all its problems.'

'Yes,' said Keith. 'No take-aways or Oxfam shops. Just the last bowling alley and the last strike.'

Only last week Nellie Jack John had gone to the Bowlorama

with a friend, without saying who it was, but that the friend had a car. Now he walked like a sick cripple.

'They're cleverer than us,' said David. 'They survived. They made an element that became extinct, that only existed for a trillionth of a second after the Big Bang, because it was made of stuff like trillionths of seconds.'

'Time,' said Keith, 'time as an element. The sort of simple thing they will discover after we become extinct. And what happened? I mean, will happen?'

'They got frightened,' said David. 'They couldn't destroy it, so they sent it away into the sea. A spider took it on a butterfly. They don't have machines, didn't have them, won't have them, shan't have them. The creature taking the element over the sea expected to be back that night, to play games, but they're still waiting for him, because he crashed.'

'Next time they'll have a machine,' said Keith. 'Butterflies aren't reliable.' He was looking at David with care and caution, in case he had indeed been teng'd by inescapable madness.

'Seriously,' said David, 'they crashed just here, about half a million years before they set off, just after the ice had melted. The butterfly is dead, but the arthropod is still about. He tried to talk to spiders first, because they were like him. But they weren't modern enough. They're still here, roaming about. I don't know what he talked to next, but the element was in the candleflame Nellie Jack John found in the cave, and the cave is at the middle of the Jingle Stones, and the Jingle Stones are there to keep Attercops in.'

'It's a good story,' said Keith, meaning that it was and that it explained some things. 'Eileen said they were a fence. Nellie Jack John puts up fences to stop the lambs going through into another time. And getting eaten by Attercops, I suppose? Or is it only a rumour?'

'The Jingle Stones are gateways,' said David.

'We know that,' said Keith. 'Is it history or futurity, or fiction?'

'It's quite simple,' said David. 'I looked in the candle, and I was trying to understand things, but I couldn't. I was a child. We were children, older than Lyddy but not so clever. Then the person, the thing before Attercop, took me through and tried to tell me what to do to get him back to his own time. I was just doing it when you came to get me, so I couldn't manage it. He's still here, and he's been trying to tell me for years what to do, but I have no idea how to manage it.'

'So we're no better off,' said Keith. 'It makes sense, but it gets us nowhere.'

They had now got to the edge of the town. It was not possible to amble along the town streets as if they were a green lane, discussing anything.

'We'll get the Land Rover,' said David. 'That'll take us somewhere. I don't know how to manage what the spider people want, but I know exactly what it is, even if there's no way of doing it.'

A few days later, alone at the Jingle Stones, David went through, and came inside the circle again at another place, seeking more knowledge and explanation.

As he stepped through the ground seized him in its dark

grip, and held him without light, his hands spread before him holding the pieces of something like shallow stone, and water bubbling through his fingers. He could neither see nor feel what he was doing, and was unable to do what he had to.

Above him someone walked, and the ground he was in quaked and quivered wetly.

But he was right to be lying here, even if he was accomplishing nothing.

OUTGANG

ONE

Keith had come out into the place he expected. He had come very warily, ready to leap back if he saw things he did not understand, between fox and spider.

He had not arrived at a time of day he expected. At first he thought the grey light was caused by his slow progress from the centre of the Jingle Stones and between two of the monoliths. He had stood for a long time in the twilight, listening. All he heard was the moorland wind dragging its way through the heather, torn and rippling, slowed and ragged. He had heard nothing else, no chatter of limbs, and seen no living back rising in the ling and sedges. He had taken five paces further into the colourless grey, and nothing had altered. Nothing moved, there was no change of light. Over to one side a deflated moon hung hazy over an indefinite horizon. Overhead, societies of alien stars brimmed bleakly in separate patches. A long way off, even further than the stars, it seemed, a raven called.

Keith turned, and was at once uncertain which stones he had passed between. But in a moment he saw his own track, where he had in some way disturbed the surface, breaking the dew that held moisture in suspension and balance, leaving a wet disorganised trace like a scar.

He went back to the beginning, through into the circle again, to the centre and his own time and place. Here there was dry daylight, a glimpse of sun, a change in the smell of the air. He was aware of distant tractors, house smoke, the uses of town five fields away. The far side there had only been empty air, uninhabited, unchanged by the making of damson jam (which Keith's mother had been doing that morning) or the purification of swimming pools (which Keith had visited with his father that morning, cold and clear).

Keith leaned on a stone and felt a little sick from hurrying back. He drew deep breaths, and that problem went away.

Another day, he thought. I shall try again. Not giving up, but I ought to go through. I can do it, I can sort it out.

He thought of Lyddy with black patches on her, patches that would not wash off in the bath. He remembered Nellie Jack John and something in a sack.

I'm not thinking of things, he decided. I can't put stories together. I have no imagination. So I can't be thinking of what I intend to do. So I'll go home and hope it goes away, because I don't like it. And I did try.

He knew that was not good enough, but when you have been feeling sick, and are uncertain of your intentions, but have to carry them out, then it is best to wait for a time and try again.

When my mind's clearer, he thought.

Before he got out of the circle again he saw the straight edge and a corner of a vehicle approaching, then the edge of the rounded roof of tractor or Land Rover. Nellie Jack John would have been a neutral visitor, but the vehicle was the Land Rover with David driving. David was coming to the Jingle Stones, the door banging, David not looking aside, David walking steadily to the circle.

Keith felt in his pockets. There was the flat blob of a wax seal found in a box at the office. There was the chalk from the game of rock chess. There were other things he might need, in one pocket and another. He marked the two stones he had been through, with little signs at the base, so that he could get back to the right place in time.

Then, before David came close enough to see him, he found the centre, and walked through a neighbouring gap out of his time and place into the moor beyond.

The town had decayed, he thought. It had shrunk back into itself. Gaps had grown among the houses. The pavements had fallen away, and grass and puddles grew among the cobbles of the marketplace. The railway station had gone. The tower of the castle had crumbled, and shops were dark and quaint.

The booths and stall of the market itself were being taken down, among puddles and grass where they stood in rows across the slope. Below the church cattle and sheep were penned. An auctioneer was singing out the prices in a gabbling psalm, and buyers were nodding out improvements in price, and making the jokes that Keith already knew. The business of the day was almost over, and the auctioneer looked round at

151

last to find there was no more to do. He waited for the church clock to strike, clouted the desk with the gavel and declared the market closed for the day. He went to help his clerk take in the money and give out receipts.

Farmers were leading their purchases away, and the streets had the traffic of hoofs in them.

Along one side of the square stood houses that Keith knew well as offices and shops. One was an inn, then as now, or now as then. Three doors away a late candle glowed behind the glass. Keith walked by and saw that nothing inside had changed, except that the candle on the desk was at another time a harsh fluorescent tube in the ceiling. His mother had often glared back at it, but nothing had been done.

It was the solicitor's office. In Keith's time that room was the reception area. In the former time it had been the office of a solicitor. He was in there now, sitting at the desk. Behind him, then as later, the black boxes that held papers and deeds and other business matters, with the client's name in gold letters on the front.

Keith knew them all. They were now empty of office papers. But he knew that the one at the bottom, on the right, held typewriter ribbons, gone dry because of what was in the next box, floppy disks and ink-jet cartridges for printers that superseded typewriters.

On the desk now stood a candle. Keith knew the computer terminal and the two telephones of his own time. Off to one side should be the photocopier, and shelves of paper.

Keith walked past the house several times. The man inside

was still there each time, writing at the desk. Keith went to see another house he knew. He did not particularly want to, and did not expect he would feel anything much about it. He had not been able to anticipate how he would feel when he stood in front of his own house. He found he was a complete stranger, totally a person with no existence, no meaning, no effect. He was pulled out of his own sense about himself, outside and in.

There were changes, but they did not matter. The side entry was blocked up now, for instance, and there was a different door at the front. More than that, he had nothing now to do with the place he had grown up in, that had known him as well as he knew it, and which now ignored him.

It is hard to be ignored by your own dwelling, that will not speak to you. It could not know him, because he was in its future. He was now in its past, though he was not sure when, and the house did not want to know. I ought to long to go in for a cup of tea, Keith thought. But Nellie Jack John had said what the dangers were of that. Besides, the people in there would be ghosts to him, something that the market folk had not been.

Walking round the town again he had not been able to find out what year it was. There were dates here and there on notices about the sales of houses, or the arrest of thieves, or their hanging, but they gave only the months and days. There was no notice that said 'This year is so and so'.

There never is, Keith thought. Bus timetables often have a note about the period they are valid, but might be a year or two old, and even bus timetables were not about now.

It feels like the future, Keith thought. It's very strange. I know it is the past, but it seems to have happened since I came through from the Jingle Stones; when I came through it was ahead of me. The houses in the gaps have not fallen down. They were never there. And someone from long ago lives in my house now, or then. Am I in now, or then; or both?

There were no street lights. The night began, and that was the end of day. Candles lit the windows facing the market place. Lanterns lighted people their way, and those people became fewer. All the hills round the town were densely black, with no glimmer of living house to be seen.

Keith went up the town, along a lane he did not know, beside fields. Here there should be houses, but he could not see them. He came to David's old house, next to the surgery and health centre, and neither of them was there. A donkey stood in the darkness and thought about things, and the lane wandered empty beyond it into the hillside empty again.

Keith walked back into the town again. This time the candle in the room had gone. There was only darkness within.

'Got to work,' Keith said to himself, almost out loud. 'What's a few hundred years?'

A few hundred years were nothing. There was only one lock on the door now, and it had always been there. Keith had used this key on it many a time. The lock worked more smoothly than he had known it, and the door opened at once.

Keith went in. He switched on the torch. It worked, across the time gap, and showed the floorboards he knew, the bare stairs beyond, and the door of the reception office. That was now a solid wooden house door, with a brass knob. At a later time it was to be glazed, with the word 'Reception' across the glass. Keith had often seen it cut the receptionist's head into shreds as she moved behind it.

The door opened when he turned the handle. There was no one inside the room, only a strange smell from the extinguished candle and farmers and paper.

The boxes were on shelves. Keith knew without looking where the SWANG FARM ESTATES box stood, because it had never been moved. Only, in Keith's day, it was empty but for the seal he had in his pocket.

Keith lifted it down and stood it on the desk. Something rattled inside it, and it hung heavier in his hands than he expected. He brought from his pocket another tool of the good burglar, a newspaper to wrap stolen goods in.

He waited and listened. Nowhere in this world did anything move, apart from the church clock opposite clanking out seven o'clock. It was so near and the town so quiet that the humming that followed seemed to last minutes. During that noise Keith unfolded the newspaper and laid it flat on the desk.

He opened the SWANG FARM ESTATES box and shone the torch into it.

There was more in there than he expected. There was a loose scroll of paper, he thought. But he felt it with his hand and knew it was parchment, with one edge scalloped and jagged, where the indenture had been cut to match it and another sheet by.

Carefully he rolled it tighter. He slipped a rubber band on it.

155

This far he had expected what he found.

The other thing in the box was a little heap of thin stones, that sounded brittle and singing when he touched them and they scraped on one another.

There was a call outside the house, out in the square. It was the night watch, passing with a lantern, and not knowing of the burglar inside the solicitor's office.

All the same, Keith's heart turned over. He felt it somersault and beat faster. He gathered up the stones, not knowing in the least what they were, chasing the last fragments round the box with his fingers, and putting everything in a jacket pocket. He closed the box, and his fingers were trembling, put it back on the shelf, took up the scroll of parchment, stowed it in an inside jacket pocket and was ready to leave.

One final flash of the torch from the doorway showed him that the SWANG FARM ESTATES box was the wrong way round on the shelf, its name to the back. But he dared not go back into the room. He left its door open. He opened the front door. No one was in sight.

He felt for the key, but it was under the noisy stones. He pulled the door to, and walked away, across the empty square, along the empty lane, past the donkey where David's old house was not, and took the road towards Swang Farm.

An hour later, stumbling in the local darkness, he missed his way among the Jingle Stones, blundering through the wrong gap.

In the middle, dazzled by daylight, he stumbled over David.

David was lying on the ground, struggling, twisting his hands, almost unable to breathe, as if a weight lay on him, or apoplexy seized him.

Keith knelt beside him, and everything was in the way, the roll of parchment being crushed against his chin, the weight of stones pulling his jacket awry. Keith took the jacket off and laid it down, to keep the parchment safe.

He turned to David, and moved him. David went on rubbing his hands together, as if he were trying to hold something.

At that moment Keith clumsily trod on the jacket, and the pocketful of stones tumbled out and fell on David's hands. Keith saw, with a sort of horror, that David had been looking for them, because the movements of his hands did not change, but now were no longer meaningless. Now, David was fitting the thin stones together, trying to make something of them. He was still unable to move the rest of himself, so that his body lay as if crushed and held. But with his hands he was fitting and holding, and making something.

Keith, unable to know what to think, in the broad daylight of a late summer's day, picked up his jacket and abandoned David, rushing out of the ring of Jingle Stones and into the darkness he had been in and felt safer in.

There, with his jaw shaking and his legs twitching, he read the chalk marks he had made. He came through into the circle, and found David sitting near the middle, putting things into his pocket.

'Be seeing you,' said David, getting up and walking away, to the Land Rover, and driving off.

Keith, feeling as if delirium had overtaken him, walked back into the town, filled again with its modern developments, and back to his house.

He felt it was glad to see him, but seeing it made him shake with emotion. He had to walk round the dusty town again before going home as if nothing had happened and it had not been rebuilt and reinhabited since he was last there, making him yet again a stranger to his own front door.

TWO

Lyddy was in the garden, red in the face and slimily blowing bubbles through a wire loop.

'Lyd,' said David, glad to see her, but not thinking about it. As time went on the gap between them seemed to grow larger, and they were no longer children together. I've grown up, he thought. She has not kept up with me.

'I'm going to fill the garden totally,' said Lyddy, splashing detergent over David. Grass clippings stuck to her cheeks, because Kirstie had been busy with the mower. 'They're up my bottom too,' she declared, scratching it to embarrass Keith.

Bubbles floated among the rose stems, and oily flowers burst on the twigs. A shimmering, shimmying, opalescent bubble lifted to eye level and hovered in front of David, its colours sliding round its surface until it dried to a dull non-colour and was no longer there, desiccating like a dream.

Dr Wix had detergent on his face, blowing bubbles to help with the grand plan.

Kirstie came out of the house. Lyddy stopped in mid blow, and a tiny bubble sank to the ground. She smiled, but the smile died as the bubble burst in the grass. They had equal and contemporary half and whole lives.

'Lyddy has something to tell David,' said Kirstie. 'Now, lassie.'

'Keith's here,' said Lyddy, changing the subject before anyone found out what it was, smiling gappily again to switch off all reproach.

'Elizabeth Clare,' said Kirstie, warningly, very Scottish, meaning danger.

'Lydia,' said David, using the serious name.

Lyddy clutched the jar of bubble stuff, and went to stand beside Keith. It seemed to her that he would be neutral, whatever happened.

'You need a lawyer,' said Kirstie. 'Right well you do.'

'My client is innocent, of course,' said Keith. 'And denies everything.'

'No, she doesn't,' said Kirstie. 'Tell David, Lyddy.'

A soapy tear ran down Lyddy's chin. A soapy bubble blistered from her nose. 'I was drawing,' she said.

'She was not near the scene of the crime,' said Keith.

'Where?' asked Kirstie. 'Tell him the scene of the crime, Lyddy.'

'On Davy's computer,' said Lyddy, and because that was guilt, waited for the sentence.

'But has hitherto led a blameless life,' said Keith.

'I never,' said Lyddy, cheering up.

'And believes there was a manufacturing defect,' Keith went on.

'It stopped working, Davy,' said Kirstie.

160

'I did it right,' said Lyddy. 'Like at school.'

'My client hung it on a hook that wasn't there,' said Keith. 'Contrary to the Health and Safety Act.'

David went indoors. His computer stood lifeless, switched off, but dry. At least there was no soapy water in it. He looked in the disk drive for biscuits, but Lyddy had not done that again. When he switched on there was a troubled cross on the screen, to say that nothing now worked.

In the garden again he said, 'It's well known. When they are one they walk, when they are two they talk, and when they are five they trash your hard disk. My hard disk. She wiped out all the information, programs, parameters, settings, internet protocols, and zapped the keyboard.'

'I'm going to bed,' said Lyddy, not admitting anything. 'I only did one thing, not all that. Keith has to bath me. He likes me.'

'In mitigation,' said Keith, 'my client says that you dropped her in the font one day, and wiped out all her information. Tut for tot. I mean tit for tat.'

'That was years ago,' said David. 'Now she goes to Gunthwait School and has new information. Like reading and writing and blowing bubbles and hacking. I expect she's brought down the whole weapons system of the northern hemisphere.'

'A fair exchange,' said Keith. 'If we are working out damages. Shall we settle out of court?'

'In a perfect world the cure for hacking is smacking,' said Kirstie.

'Not a perfect world,' said Lyddy. 'Things break.' She put her tongue up one nostril – she could do that – and licked away runniness, swallowing it thoughtfully.

You've got to forgive her, David thought, remembering her dressed in white at Whitsun in Gunthwait chapel, like a stranger angel, singing madrigals; and then coming home to eat baked potato with jam; the sister that cried at school on her first day because her brother was not there and she had not dreamed his school was a different one.

It's the way they bring them up, Keith decided.

She's bringing herself up, thought David. I knew I had a sister, but not that it was her.

Have to make allowances; but I won't bath her, Keith concluded. 'She'd splash me,' he said.

'I'll do it, very cruelly,' said David. He meant quickly. 'Then Keith can read to you if the words aren't very long, while I see to the computer.'

'More of that funny story about parties,' said Lyddy. 'It was cool, I didn't have to listen.'

'I'll write it down,' said Keith. 'If you'll lend me some ink.'

'You'll need the feathers as well,' said Lyddy.

'Just take it, Keith,' said Kirstie. 'But take care too. They made it at school and since then all her clothes look as if they're wanting washed.'

'Nellie Jack John brought a bag of apples to school,' Lyddy remembered. 'They grow on oak trees but they're not acorns.'

'Or PCs,' said David.

THREE

David had gathered up the shaly stones as they whispered in his hands, wafers of sound that meant nothing and everything. Then Keith had appeared, and had not to see them.

David did not understand why, only that it was so. Long ago, when Nellie Jack John had brought the candle out of the hill, David had looked into that flame with the same private urge, and that had been deadly, without resolving into the end of things.

Now the gathering of stones held some similar personal message, for David's hands alone.

The sense of being in the hill, under the peat, merging with the theophany, left him. He had only evening round him, and something in his hands.

'Be seeing you,' he told Keith, and went to the Land Rover.

He had not felt like saying anything more in any case, after an experience he could not understand either, of being buried in deep moss, in the forming peat that had once buried the Jingle Stones.

In that peat, in that underground, had been the cave. In the centre of the cave had been the stones, which had to be put together to make something.

If I understood, David thought. I have seen the pictures, but it is like reading a comic in another language. I do not know whether it says 'Zap' or 'I love you'. The pictures are not sense by themselves. I do not know the motives of anyone.

But the pictures are the instructions for the stones.

As well as that, he had an irrelevant thought, in the way that things approach each other without belonging. The thought was about the lease and the rent cup, which were matters related only in the way they came to his notice, not in real terms.

They did not influence each other, only interfered in tiresome ways with no effect but muddle.

The stones lay in a drawer for a long time. Even Lyddy had no interest in them after she had scraped them together ten times to make their brittle sound.

They're important, David thought. But not interesting, which is contrary of them. Even the brightness faded, and they no longer held light, only reflected it solidly the darker the night, the brighter the source shone on them.

One day, baby-sitting on a wet evening, he was playing cards with Lyddy, so that she could beggar-her-neighbour with all determination. Then she wanted to play strip-poker, with Gytrash as a player.

Instead David built her a two-storey card house, which Gytrash huffed down by merely looking at it.

Lyddy had then gone to get the stones, and built with them a little cave, because they were thin and had shapes that might fit together.

With a lot of propping up and fumbling she made a jar that collapsed immediately. For a moment it existed, but then could not be remade. Lyddy pushed the pieces away and left them.

I am being childish too, David thought, in keeping them. My mind is still irrational.

But he put them back in the drawer, because he still had in his mind pictures that might be holding a meaning for them.

There are more pieces, he thought. I cannot put it together. But he kept what he had.

FOUR

The writing was very easy to imitate, Keith found. In fact it was the only old-fashioned script he could do. The feathers Lyddy had given him with the ink were difficult, and a steel pen gave the wrong effect. He stole a quill from a decoration in the sitting room at home, and cut it on a taper and split it.

'What is this black on your shirt cuff?' his mother said. 'I can't get it out. Have you been taking notes in court?'

Keith thought about courts as he rubbed out with a pumice stone from the bath-tub and wrote in new words. 'This is illegal,' he told himself. 'Probably. But it is right. And I can't tell anyone about it.'

One day in September, in the time when David had left school and had not yet gone up to the university, the job was finished, and the agreement carefully dated. The ink was drying away too, and the quill blunt and softening, but the matter was now clear and must settle all arguments.

'It must be right,' he told himself out loud. 'I shall gain nothing from it. But it is still illegal.'

'You are working too hard,' his mother said. 'I know the exams are important, but you do not need to hurry.'

166

'No hurry at all,' said his father. 'When he passes them the firm will have to pay him more for making the same mistakes.'

Keith had to wait for an opportunity to replace the scroll, because the exam work had hardly been touched. Rain kept falling that year, and on fine days there were other things to deal with, such as the exams themselves.

I need help, Keith thought, but I can't ask David. I can't ask anyone. He went through one of his arguments again, about putting the scroll back in its box in the present day. But that would not do because it had to be out of the way before Keith himself was born, as his alibi. How could he have had anything to do with it? It must be impossible for him to have encountered it.

On a dry overcast evening he went up to the Jingle Stones, with the scroll, the key, a torch, and some old money, in case he had expenses.

He went through at the place he knew, and found himself in the morning of the other side. The sun was coming up in the east, and the church clock, when he heard it at the edge of the town, struck seven.

Good thing about money, he thought, seeing a long and hungry day ahead. Then he remembered that he could not eat here, or he would be locked in for seven years.

In the end he did not stay long. There was turmoil in the town, with bugles blowing, a column of men marching untidily down a muddy road, a cow being chopped up at the cross-roads, and a group of people being rounded up by soldiers.

At the head of the lane where the surgery would one day be,

there were uniformed sentries. They saw him and shouted. One of them raised a gun, slowly, slowly, until Keith could no longer see it foreshortened against the man's shoulder. There was a puff of smoke, then a crack from the gun and at the same time something slapped like a dropped hammer against a tree beside Keith. Bark stuck out at random angles, and he smelt sap. Drops of rain showered from the leaves of the branches overhead

Keith knew better than to stay. He stepped aside into cover, and scrambled over a dry stone wall, running low behind it, scuttled like Attercop over another, and hurried back towards the Jingle Stones.

No one followed him.

There is a revolution, he thought. I started it last time I was here. I have interfered with history. I caused the War of the Spanish Succession by changing something trivial. It says so in all the books. I am guilty of forging actuality.

When he sat down to take a breath he realised that whatever had happened would already have done so, by the time he got home. Things had come round to what he already knew, or could find out. If in going he had altered anything then it must have been necessary before he went back.

Now, with his breath in order, his heart working tranquilly, he could hardly recall which side of time he was. The hillside looked exactly the same. 'I have got back,' he told a cloud of midges all spaced out and orderly in their unplanned way. 'I can go to Swang and see Eileen and get a cup of tea. I mustn't show the lease agreement, that's all. I'll go back into town another day.'

Swang was just over the brow of a hill. Keith smelt tractor smoke in his mind before he was over the top. But it did not last.

Swang was a long low house, with a yard and buildings behind it, and beside it a garden patch and an orchard; and generally smoke at the chimney, a streak of torn earth at the back gate, and a dog broadcasting from a kennel.

Keith could deal with the town. He had come to terms with his own house acting indifferently towards him. He had expected changes there, and accepting them as part of history, a future-feeling past. His surroundings were now so familiar that he forgot he was out of his own time, that Eileen would not be at Swang, that real time had an overcast sky and was going on for darkness.

He was not ready for Swang to be a tangle of briars, a sunken roof, a single standing end wall, a yard with a tumbled barn; no smoke, no sound, no habitation. Moss had invaded the kitchen floor, across the stone flags. Sunshine coloured the moss, living there as the only inhabitant.

The sight hit him like death. He understood the sense of it, that this was long ago, that the Swang he knew was real for him at the end of the twentieth century and must have recovered. He knew that, and could rely on it. But the vision of it broken and abandoned hurt him more than almost anything ever had.

He had to go down there and look more closely. He felt it was an indecent thing to pry and peer at the desolation, but he was impelled to look, forced to tread there, bound to lift the brambles aside and see the kitchen he knew, the very fireplace and grate he had often sat by, was often to sit by.

But he could not resist the urge to be there, to feel the anguish for times past and yet-to-come twisting physically in his chest and behind his eyes, while he stood inside the broken walls with upstair and downstair windows that looked either side to the sky, and mourned the rubble that sloped from the derelict wainscots.

Scrambling over walls he had lost the handkerchief from his trouser pocket. But he needed it, because there were tears in his eyes. They hardly expressed what he felt, but he knew it would take him a lifetime to understand that. For him, from now on, Swang would always appear somewhat destroyed, wounded in its reality, and he would always feel grief for that.

All history is that, he knew, finding a rather posh silk handkerchief in his top jacket pocket and using it. There was another heave of tears, and then it was over and only his nose ran.

He sat a little longer on a heap of stone, and wondered how to overcome the loneliness the building must now have. He thought of a way, and he had the means to provide it.

He found twigs and windfall branches everywhere. He heaped up a little-pig house in the hearth, struck a match, and lit the house. Heat snapped, and sunshine that would never reach the hearth in Keith's day hid the flames. But smoke went up, and warmth reached out to him, and smoke to wet his eyes again.

The house, Swang Farm, felt better again, and he felt calmer.

I can't go into town, he thought. I can't get the lease into its box. I know it got there in some way or other or my grandfather would not have sent it to the Land Deeds Registry office before I was born. But I have it here in my inside pocket, rolled up into a tube and touching my neck, all made out clearly and perfectly and signed and dated, and the seal that fell off it some time but is loose in my pocket . . . But the seal was not there. All the same, Keith knew, it had survived, and did not now matter.

Nor does it matter what I do with the lease, Keith realised. It turns up again, so it must survive.

Except, of course, an indenture was called that from having both copies with the same randomly cut edge, sometimes joining together laid out flat, other times one laid on the other, to prove that both sides agreed.

The copy he had might not be the one in the Land Deeds Registry, Keith now knew. And wondered why he had not known that all along. The future may not be the future I expect. I may have done all this forgery in vain. I have been wicked to no purpose. Even Lyddy is not wicked on purpose.

It must be the ink, he thought; but I don't make jokes. Except, I am thinking of one now.

He turned his back on the fire, like a householder, and looked about him. One day in the future the lease must be found. It is made of very tough stuff. If I wanted to hide it to be discovered at a future date . . . discovered by me . . . on the date at the end of the lease . . . in this very room where we shall all discuss it in a couple of years' time . . . where would I put it?

This was a room he knew, in a house he knew, even if the main part of the walls had fallen.

Was there a place in the remainder of the walls? Under the stone sill of the window?

The flags of the floor were covered in rubble. Ash trees grew in corners, and grass at the hearth where Eileen's stobbed rug would later lie.

Round the corner, through an empty doorway, Keith found what he was looking for. A ragged flight of stone steps went down into a cellar he had not known about, and sunlight broke through from a crumbled wall at the far side.

He went down carefully. The stone steps had slipped and subsided, but brought him down to a floor that was clearer than the kitchen floor above, which held so much fallen roof.

The cellar had house wall on three sides, and at the back the living rock of the hillside, with an entry like a cave in it.

Sunlight came in from the east, where that wall had become delapidated, and filled the cellar like a fire.

In here, Keith thought, so certain that he already had the document out of his pocket ready in his hand before he found the right place.

There were smaller cavities too in the rock wall. One of them was deep enough, and dry enough, for the length of the roll.

He wrapped the parchment in his elegant silk handkerchief with his tears on it, tucking the ends in. It was like a bright Christmas cracker before it has been crimped.

He pushed it into the hole. As he did so there was a glint of light deep in the rock, and a resistance. He pulled the tube out again, and cleaned cobwebs from the end. The soft but dusty silk had not kinked the end of the tube. He put it in again.

There was soft resistance still, but he knew what it was, and pushed the parchment fully in, its full length, and then wrist deep.

There was another glint of light, and something ran over his wrist. His hand came out of the hole on its own accord, whether he wanted it or not. A great spider fluttered on the back of his hand. Its eyes flashed in the sunlight, and it dropped to the floor. He saw it rear up and threaten him.

'Attercop,' he said, to tease it. Then wished he had not said it, put in this ruined farmhouse in the past of his own time.

The spider scuttled across the cellar floor.

Sunlight dropped away, but for some reason Keith could not understand the rock itself did not lose any brightness, as if it had residual luminosity.

He had nearly finished, and wanted to be away.

For good measure he put in the coins he had brought with him, the aluminium torch as a proper scientific experiment, his Swiss Army knife, and from the bottom of his pocket a circular stone that had been with the lease and not slipped out at the middle of the Jingle Stones when the rest had; but it belonged with the parchment; and that was all he had. David would have devised something better, he knew.

He blocked the end of the hole with three stones. The last one fitted snugly in the cavity, and no one who did not know there was a reason to remove it would trouble to take it out, because it matched the stratification of the rock.

The sunlight faded. Keith climbed the cellar stair and came

into the kitchen again. His fire had gone out. His day this side of time was over. He had no more business here.

He made his way cautiously to the Jingle Stones. Somewhere down by the town there was gunfire, and the bugle still called.

His chalk marks were still in place. There was no sign of any large Attercop. Among the Jingle Stones he stood for a moment with morning at one hand and evening at the other, and came through into the overcast evening. He dusted a fragment of web from his sleeve and went home.

'Goodness,' said his mother. 'You smell of smoke. Not like cigarettes, I hope.'

'Bonfire,' said Keith. 'At Swang.'

FIVE

'You should have come to Bulgaria with me,' said David.

Keith was puffing a bit on the hill. David had made him walk to the summit of Jingle Fell, on the look-out for Lyddy, who was lost nearly to the point of being looked for.

'I have to sit at a desk every day,' said Keith. 'And you live miles up at Crackpot when you aren't in wherever it is, studying whatever they are, and sending me hieroglyphic postcards of ruins.'

'Cyrillic,' said David. 'The postcards.'

Keith sat on a rock and looked at the nearby ground. David stood on the same rock and looked at all Vendale below, resting in its own groove, sometimes hidden by its own crookedness, often flinging a rocky limb up into the hills, green with summer to come, blue with grounded sky in the low still river.

To the east there was the smoke of the town, the houses invisible behind a ridge. To the west stood a distant palisade of lake mountains.

'Look at something,' said David. 'You are dreaming internally on the top of the hill with the whole world to look at.'

'I've never been anywhere,' said Keith.

'You've been in stranger places than this,' said David. 'As abroad as anywhere.'

'Me?' said Keith.

He's no good at lying, David thought. But then you never had a little sister to observe and practise on. 'You went with me through the Jingle Stones,' said David. 'I saw you after that, making chalk marks, coming and going. We've both been into some place yonder, years ago, not long ago; and you've been again by yourself and saying nothing.'

'Client confidentiality,' said Keith, changing the course of the enquiry.

'The witness must answer my questions,' said David, without wanting to push Keith the wrong way at all. 'You'll get to be an M.P. if you don't look out. Did he or did he not go through to that other place more than once without reporting the fact to the proper authorities?'

'There aren't any proper authorities,' said Keith. 'Oh, you mean you?'

'The authority on having gone in yonder and coming back,' said David.

'Without knowing anything about it,' said Keith.

'I know stuff,' said David. 'But it wasn't stuff that happened to me over there. It happened to someone or something else in another place entirely, and I was just told it. I was fed it. It was put in my memory bank, bits and pieces, they don't mean much, they don't connect. I think they're dead, because it's all gone away, but it isn't complete. I didn't know how to help.'

176

'Attercop stuff,' said Keith. They both thought about that, and about Nellie Jack John.

'Still got a bad leg,' said David. 'From that bite. And Gytrash bit him in the same place. But what about you going through into that other place?'

'There's your Mum getting to Swang,' said Keith. 'We'd better go down.'

'Don't change the subject,' said David. 'The question is whether you did what you did, or was it some other person?'

'That?' said Keith, 'Them?'

'Whatever,' said David.

'I didn't see Attercop again,' said Keith. 'Yes, I went through several times. The town hasn't changed much, but it's quite different. Our offices were still there, but the woolclip office was being built. There were wasps' nests and soldiers in the castle, and homeless huts by the walls.'

'But you didn't hear about Attercop, or anything?' said David.

'I just looked,' said Keith. 'That's all.'

'And solicitors don't lie,' said David.

'Not so's you'd notice,' said Keith.

'I get bothered when they tell the truth,' said David.

Keith had his breath back by now. 'We haven't been up here for seven years or so,' he said. 'We used to walk a million miles a day and never notice. Also, we didn't look at anything properly. But now I know where places are. That's Swang Farm down there. There's a tractor in the home field. Nellie Jack John came down in March to pay the rent. They still do that. There's things I can't say about the rent. I wish I could. Working it out is horrendous, but now we're convinced nobody cares. We are convinced there is nobody to do the caring.'

'Eileen does,' said David. 'But it's all so cloudy, nothing works. Now we're not children any more, and we can work things out, the less meaning they have.'

Keith understood that, and how going on a million miles these days got you nowhere new. 'My mother says you just have to go on ploating life's fowl,' he said. 'And let the feathers float away.'

'Better find the little beast,' said David. 'And pull out a few feathers. Sometimes she's so awful she must have been on a course for it.'

'She doesn't know which way is north,' said Keith. 'She told me she only knew about yesterday.'

'I'm trying to hate her,' said David, 'because I don't have to love her, but I do.'

He looked at the ring of Jingle Stones, high above Swang, far along this same hillside, lying on it like Lyddy's broken seven-year-old smile. On this hill they had once seen giants walking. David did not wonder about giants, but why the hill was covered in grass and heather, with a ring of stones on it; and whether the ring had invisible neighbours.

'Has your father still got that black Jeep?' said Keith, because David was mumbling to himself, in what might be Bulgarian, Keith thought. 'He's just coming up the track to the house, and there's a dog and a girl standing up in the sunroof.'

'Tea time,' said David. 'You're quite right: we used to go all over the place here, but we didn't see the importance of things.

We knew the Jingle Stones had been put there for some reason, and thought that the being there was more important than the reason. That must be the wrong way round – the reason is more important.'

'When Frank's father took one of the stones away a boggart began rushing about the house,' said Keith. 'Did that happen in Bulgaria?'

'Every day,' said David. 'They're still sending out boggart relief schemes.'

'In Cyrillic,' said Keith.

'We'll go up in your car,' said David.

SIX

'You never send me the ruins of a postcard,' said Lyddy. She was busy packing her school bag. A year or two earlier David might have known what should go in it. He had a guess now.

'Reading folder,' he said, but Lyddy said she had done reading and wasn't going to school, do you mind, Day-vidd, it was her own business, and My Little Pony is next, can't leave it.

'Oh, picnic,' said David, seeing food going in after the pink creature. 'And swimming.'

'Just knickers,' said Lyddy. 'I wouldn't swim topless.'

Of course it's logic, David told himself, she doesn't have a two-piece; and left her to it. She was not quite cross, but had decided to do something that would not be allowed, when her father and Kirstie were out, so David had to keep her under observation, on a very wet summer's day. There was no going outside. He decided that Lyddy was probably only having activity, or hyperactivity, or contrariness.

The telephone rang.

'It's for me,' said Lyddy. 'Hello,' she said. 'Oh, Keith, I wasn't expecting you, I'm not in,' and put the telephone back on its hook. 'Not for me,' she said.

Keith was used to her telephone manner. He had stayed on the line. David picked the telephone up and found him still there, explaining about weather.

'Really foul up here too,' said David.

'After milking,' Keith said. 'You'd think it would be a decent day. I've always thought it would be, but it isn't. I hope it goes right, because bad weather makes things worse.'

'You're the one that knows how it will go,' said David. 'You haven't said anything about it for years, but you couldn't tell me then and you can't tell me now.'

Lyddy picked up another telephone and snorted into it, which was just her way of breathing secretly. 'Keith,' she said.

'Yes,' said Keith.

'Shut up,' said Lyddy. 'Don't tell David, but I'm going to do something exciting. Then you can come and tell us a story.'

'It might have a sad ending,' said Keith.

'And funny,' said Lyddy. She had finished talking, but went on listening with all her breath.

'O.K. Keith,' said David, in a heavy tone. 'We'll say goodbye now shall we,' leaving out all question marks and intonations.

Lyddy got off the line, and went on rummaging in a cupboard, without putting the telephone back, so she could be heard chatting to herself. Keith had understood the subjunctives of David's speech and was still holding on. 'Yes,' he said.

'She wants a little friend,' said David. 'But she's only got me.'

'After milking,' said Keith. 'Did I say? Be there. My dad is coming up. I'm not sure about anything, the lease, the rent, the rent cup, nothing.'

'Talk again,' said David. 'I'm stuck here all day with Elizabeth,' and rang off.

Keith had said 'Rent cup,' darting the word at David out of nowhere, and for no clear reason.

But that is not how reason works. Reason is one of the random effects of apparent confusion and chance. So Keith's chance remark, meaning nothing to Keith, had meaning for David.

Lyddy was putting her yellow mac on, and looking annoyingly cute.

'If you're going out,' said David, 'brush your hair.' She knew she was not going out, but she brushed her hair. David left her to it and got out the flat stones. Lyddy heard them chinking and came to help.

'They can't be anything,' said David, finding no meaning or structure in them. 'I'll take them to Swang later on.'

'I'm going that way,' said Lyddy. 'I'll take them, shall I? I haven't got room today, though.'

Her school bag was full, and the flap tied down hard. There was a scatter of biscuit crumbs round it, and her yellow rain hat on top.

'You're not going out,' said David.

'I brushed my hair,' said Lyddy.

Dr Wix and Kirstie were back by four o'clock. David gave up the baby sitting responsibility and began to sort some co-ordinates on the computer. Lyddy read them out to him inaccurately for a time, then wandered away. David went on for a while, then began to finger the stones again. He wondered what kind of stone they were, man-made or natural, and where from. I might at least have found that out, he thought. I'll take them down. They can't be anything, but I'll put them in my pocket and take them.

Lyddy had escaped, with no one watching her. The long rain across the landscape hindered vision, but David thought he saw the yellow mac far down the lane, and Gytrash bounding from side to side, helping Lyddy along.

'She said she was going to Swang,' he told Kirstie. The schoolbag was missing. 'I think she's planning to stay there.'

She had stayed overnight before, and expected breakfast in bed, so it was better than home.

'I'll ring later,' said Kirstie. 'Your father's on the telephone just now. She's a wicked bairn. If she was minded to go, I'm surprised you kept her in the house while we were out.'

Lyddy knew where she was going, and why. She had failed once, and was not going to fail this time; or if she did, she would do the final thing, and that would show them not to stop her being reasonable. After all, reason is just luck, Davy said.

The school bag was too full and banging on her rump. But all the things would be needed, and what she hadn't got Eileen would provide. Eileen did the right things, bacon all bubbly, and fires all day.

Keith said, 'No, she's not here. Is she, Eileen? Lyddy.'

'Not today,' said Eileen, thinking of other things. 'Not

expecting her. I was wondering, what'll we do about that little grave, David, if we have to go, that child and her toy in the ground alone with strangers? Is your father coming, Keith?'

'Yes,' said Keith, drying his head on a towel. 'He had to go to Durham, but he'll come straight on when he gets back.'

'We'll wait for him,' said Frank. 'It's better from him, good or bad, Keith.'

Keith could not say anything. Goodness or badness depended on the lease document, and he could not tell anyone where it was.

'I'd better ring Mum,' said David. 'We were sure Lyddy was here. She said she would be, and she might go her own way but wouldn't tell a lie. She wouldn't be going anywhere else and say it was here, but she might still be somewhere else and not have got here yet, which she hasn't.'

Nellie Jack John was wondering, he said, why Keith was here, if his father was to do the job. 'It doesn't take two to shear a sheep,' he said. 'Unless it's a bigger yowe than we bargain for. But Keith's, like, grinning, even if he tries to hide it.'

'Well, I expect it'll be . . .' Keith began. But before he finished his sentence the back door of Swang was pushed open and slammed shut. An instant later there was a jumping in the ceiling, enough for dust to come down.

'Boggart,' said David. He could talk to boggarts and tame them slightly.

'It's the latch,' said Eileen. 'It should have been fettled, but maybe it's past its time for us.'

The room door opened. Lyddy came in, dripping with rain,

184

pulling off her hat, and grinning. 'We're hungry,' she said. 'We've finished the biscuits.'

Alec-Edward followed her. He had not changed in a year or so, though last time he had been dry and now he was wet through. He was smiling solemnly and eating a limp biscuit.

'Eh well, what'll we do?' said Eileen. 'Who's the lile lad? Come by, love, and let the fire dry you. You mother won't want you home with a cold.'

'I'm his mother,' said Lyddy. 'I don't care if he's wet.'

'Lyddy,' said David, 'we'll have to take him back again before he has anything to eat. Eileen, I'd better ring home. Don't take your coat off, Lyddy.' But she had already hung it on the floor.

'He won't hurt for a bite to eat and some hot tea in him,' said Eileen, rubbing Alec-Edward's head with the towel Keith had finished with.

Dr Wix's Jeep pulled into the yard then, before David got to the telephone.

'Too many folk,' said Nellie Jack John, meaning Lyddy and Alec-Edward. 'I ken who he is. That's my uncle that Attercop got before I was born. She's been over there and taken him.'

Alec-Edward was looking round and beaming at all the company. He pushed Lyddy away, because she was not interesting now that he saw real food on the table.

'He's a great eater,' said David.

'And that,' said Keith, remembering his shoes.

Dr Wix and Kirstie came in, enquiring for Lyddy.

'She's here,' said Frank, while Eileen mopped at Alec-

Edward's head. 'There's room for all, and Mr Heseltine is coming up for the last rent, and it's like a farewell party, I doubt.'

Kirstie was looking at Lyddy, and at Alec-Edward. 'Let me get this right,' she said. 'Is this your friend you brought before, Lyddy?'

Lyddy nodded her head, pleased but apprehensive. She clutched the end of the towel she had dried her face with.

'And what did we tell you?' said Kirstie. 'Eileen, I'm sorry, but there is going to be a muckle row, so we'll take her right away at once, and deal with her at home. And it's no good smiling, Lyddy, because you are seriously out of line and I am going to be angrier with you than any mother has ever been with a seven-year-old who is totally disobedient. So come along with you now, and I'll talk to you at home. David, will you deal with this other child? You did it last time.'

Lyddy's eyes filled with tears. She did not sob, but flooded. Her face became pink and white, and round her eyes appeared a pale bruising. She stood, and breathed in her throaty way, but otherwise wept in silence. The face that had just been wiped dry became wet all over, as if she wept through her skin, and her shirt became soaked in tears. She said nothing, and stood in pitiable terror.

Outside, Gytrash began to howl. With support from him the tears ran faster.

'But,' said Eileen, 'where's he from? There aren't any houses between here and Crackpot.'

'He'll not get back,' said Nellie Jack John, 'if he eats owt else.'

There was a knock at the front door of the house. Someone

outside was complaining quietly. It was not Keith's father's voice.

'I'll git t'door,' said Nellie Jack John, lifting his head and looking smugly pleased.

'Oh yes, John,' said Eileen. 'She'll be so wet.'

Nellie Jack John went out of the kitchen and down the passage to the front door and pulled it open.

'I was telling him,' the visitor said, 'I told him, John, not this door.'

'Some folk don't know,' said Nellie Jack John. 'Come by, Sally. And thou.'

'The person called Metcalfe,' said Dr Tate, following her into the room. 'She was walking up, and I was coming to see whether you needed a local historian to give you a hand. I hear it's a critical day.'

'It's what I call a kitchen,' said Sally, shaking rain from her hair. 'You don't feel you're in the country, more like on telly.' She went to sit next to Nellie Jack John. He looked like the cat that won its way on to your lap.

'Sithee,' he said, and put his hand on the shelf beside the kitchen fire, picked something up and gave it to Sally.

Sally opened the plastic Safeway bag. She took out a pair of slim grey gloves. 'Silk,' she said. 'Where did you get them, John?'

'Knit 'em,' said Nellie Jack John. 'I looked at thy fingers to geg t'size, and it's Attercop silk off t'moor, and we could all knit owt in my time. Will ta tek them?'

'Aye,' said Sally. 'Aiblins,' meaning the perhaps that was a certainty. She slid the gloves on and off, wrapped them in their bag again, and held them.

Lyddy snorted and went to stand next to Keith. Outside, the rain beat on the window. Keith sat on the stone sill beneath it, and a cold draught beat on the back of his knees. Lyddy wiped her nose on her sleeve and looked at Sally and Nellie Jack John. 'Hand in love,' she said.

'Attercop?' said Dr Tate. 'Is that tea?'

'Reach to,' said Eileen. 'Take what's here, and welcome. I don't know what sort of a party this is, but we'll make the best of it. We've just to wait for Mr Heseltine, and we'll know. He didn't know this morning, so I hope he does when he comes.'

'Well, said Keith, 'we don't need to wait for him, Eileen. I think I can solve the problem just by sitting here.' Then he looked uncomfortable, because every eye in the room looked at him.

'What dost mean, thou daft beggar?' said Nellie Jack John. 'What's thy arse to do wi' t'job?'

Keith took a breath, swallowed, coughed, and said as calmly as he could, 'The lease document is in the cellar under this room, wrapped in a silk handkerchief.'

Frank looked at Keith. 'Is this right?' he asked.

'How do you know? asked Eileen, her hand at her throat.

'What's he on about?' said Sally.

Alec-Edward crept forward and took a sausage roll.

'Now, Keith,' said Dr Wix, 'this isn't like you to make senseless jokes.'

'The only kind he knows,' said David. 'Isn't it, Keith?'

'In the cellar under here,' said Keith. 'The lease document.'

Frank shook his head. 'I don't what it is wi' thee, Keith, but I've lived here all my life, and my dad before me, and I know there's no cellar to the house, under this room or any.'

SEVEN

'No cellar,' said Eileen. 'Keith.'

'Keith?' said Dr Tate.

Keith felt that he had been hit over the heart with a shovel, a big flat blow. His breath curdled in his lungs. It had been going to be a finer moment, he had thought, not the pressure of so many other people, not Lyddy hanging on to his sleeve, not the accusation of playing with people's feelings and futures and talking rank insanity. He could not speak. He could not stand. His mind was in a turmoil of knowing he was right, and not being able to believe its own functions.

Alec Edward seized a scone.

'It can't be the right answer, Keith,' said Dr Tate. 'But it's not like you to take leave of your senses.'

'I haven't,' said Keith, at last. 'There's a cellar under this floor.' Don't cry, he told himself. Grown-up person. Drop dead ugly. Only hunks cry.

'You'd best hope so,' said Frank. 'It's best to be right, Keith,' he said. 'But I've known thee many years, and I'll give you the best of the doubt until I learn not to.'

'It's there,' said Keith, gulpingly. 'Under our feet.'

'Thou kens ower mich,' said Nellie Jack John. 'And nowt.'

'Is it always like this here?' asked Sally.

'He won't do it again,' said Nellie Jack John. 'He won't be here another time.'

Eileen was at the fire, teapot in one hand, kettle in the other, frozen as she occupied herself instead of merely watching, but unable to continue what she was doing.

'Cellar,' said Frank. 'It's time thy Dad took thee away, Keith, and God help you.'

'I've known this boy a long time,' said Dr Tate. 'He's frequently been an idiot, but not a liar.'

'Cellar!' said Frank.

Dr Tate began to walk about the room, stamping his feet. 'Just listen,' he said. 'Is there a different sound in the middle? Under the table.'

'I'm not moving the table,' said Frank. 'I'm bloody not. It's never been moved. There's no trapdoor there – you can see the flags; they've never been shifted, and I know it.'

Keith had managed to stand up. His knees were trembling and his hands shook. 'I thought you'd know,' he said, his voice croaking.

'I do,' said Frank.

'How to get down there,' said Keith, leaning against the table and walking to the far door of the room. He wanted to say he had been there, through the doorway; the doorway that he would show them.

'Just a passage,' said Eileen. 'To the front door.'

Keith could hardly breathe. He took himself out of the

kitchen door, and looked for the doorway to the cellar steps.

There was a plain plastered wall, with wallpaper smooth across it. He ran a frail hand across it. 'Here,' he said.

Dr Tate was still banging his heel on the kitchen floor. 'Some resonance,' he said.

'By God,' Frank was saying, 'tha knaws summat, Keith.'

'We had it plastered,' said Eileen. 'Just that bit.'

'It was an old wall,' said Frank. 'Rough as bags. We can get it plastered again. If.'

Nellie Jack John had left the kitchen, gone out of the house, and came back with a sledgehammer. 'You'll need to,' he said. 'If.'

'No "If",' said Keith, in a failed whisper like a cough.

'Don't make a mess,' said Eileen. 'It'll be in the deeds, that's what, Frank. It's in the deeds, the lease, Keith, isn't it?'

'Mother!' said Nellie Jack John. 'Get a wheelbarrow and a shovel. It'll not be a mess but a tip.'

He swung the sledgehammer, awkwardly because the passage restricted him, and knocked a crater into the plaster. He struck again, and a third time.

The plaster stayed in place. But behind the wall a stone fell out backwards, hit the ground below, and then walked, one step at a time, down to the bottom of the cellar stairs.

Frank and Eileen looked at one another. Eileen looked apprehensive, her mouth open, as if something she knew about had happened again. Frank nodded his head, to show that something was now explained.

'If it's just that,' he said. 'Just a cellar, then it's all right, Eileen.'

Nellie Jack John swung again at the same spot. The head of the sledgehammer sank into the wall this time, and rested there, not swinging back. There was a lumpy rustle of falling dry plaster. There was the thud of falling stone. A pebble danced away into the depths, tap, tap, tappety tap, rolled, and stood silent.

'Give me yon sledge,' said Frank.

Before he handed it over Nellie Jack John pounded the head of it against the wall like a battering ram, bringing down plaster, ripping paper away with his hands, dust coming out in a dry fountain. A cool dry breeze brimmed out of the black hole he had made, full of dust and grit, welling out almost visibly, making torn fronds of wallpaper at the edge of the hole lift like the tentacles of anemones.

Frank slammed the sledgehammer against the lower edge of the wall. No one in that narrow passage spoke, mostly because of the dust getting at their throats. In the room behind Lyddy was saying, 'I can't pour the tea, Alec-Edward, the teapot's too heavy,' and Alec-Edward was eating the whole dish of hard-boiled eggs.

'And then what, Keith?' Dr Wix was asking, standing back, leaving Frank room to wield the hammer.

'The deed is down there,' said Keith. 'Parchment and stuff.'

'You canna ken it,' said Kirstie. 'How can you?'

'Keith?' said David. 'You understand the question.'

Keith's confusion had begun to leave him. How he knew something did not matter. The cellar was being found. Even Dr Tate had stopped trying to prove it by stamping on the floor, now that certainty had taken its place. Keith cleared his throat, but not entirely of dust.

'Client confidentiality,' he said.

'That?' said Kirstie, meaning that she would have it out of him later, and that he would be easier to crack than Lyddy.

Lyddy, in the kitchen, was tempting Alec-Edward to salad dressing.

'I'll get t'lantern,' said Nellie Jack John, when Frank had opened a hole large enough to get his shoulders through.

'No need,' said Frank, coming back out of the cavity. 'There's daylight coming in.'

'Where from?' asked Eileen. 'There isn't a window anywhere.'

'Don't ask me,' said Frank. 'I can see, so it's daylight. Away, Nellie, and pull out these stones, and I'll get down. There's steps here.'

Nellie Jack John pulled at stones, kicking and hitting.

'I never gave you credit, Keith,' said Frank. 'I don't know how you knew owt about it, but you've got old plans at the office, I doubt. I wonder your Dad didn't tell us about it, or his Dad before him.'

He didn't know, thought Keith. I'll explain later, when we've got the deed out and sorted everything.

Frank opened the front door again, the second time that day, possibly the second time that year. He began to throw rock and rubble out of it. Then he went out and looked at the house from outside.

'No windows,' he said, coming in again. 'Not down there.' Then he pushed Nellie Jack John to one side, a remaining stone to the other, and bent low to get through the hole in the wall.

'It's a doorway,' he said. 'Here's the door leaning against the back wall, and steps going down.'

The upwelling breeze had stopped now. Frank put a foot on the top step.

'Frank, be careful,' said Eileen.

'I'll gan with him,' said Nellie Jack John. 'Eh?'

Keith had got back his composure. He had got more than that. He was assured of being right, of success, and knew that in a moment he would recover the parchment and so astonish the world still more. 'I'll go with him,' he said. 'I know what I'm doing. David.'

'I don't know what you're doing,' said David. 'I don't even know what I'm doing.'

'I'm off after them, Mother,' said Nellie Jack John.

Eileen looked doubtful about that. Dr Wix said, 'If it's the cellar to this house it's not about to fall in on them. Anything else and you have a trained medical team on hand.'

'It'll be all right,' said Keith. He had one doubt he could not resolve, which concerned the light below that cast Frank's shadow back up the steps.

And for David the shadows were reminiscent of other shadows, other places underground. This time, though, there was no sudden flood of memory too strong to be tasted, but a cool recognition that here there might be an answer, a clarification, a resolution.

He followed Nellie Jack John into the shadows, into the light.

The steps were solid but irregular. At the foot of them lay newly fallen stone from the wall.

The light was from everywhere, not big, not bright, casting shadows only up the steps, because in the cellar itself it was almost without direction. They all stood and accustomed themselves to it, and then could see.

The floor was covered with elderly rubbish, firewood, coal, broken derelict chairs, pieces of iron kitchen equipment from a previous century – or the century before that, considering the date this year.

Keith was counting his way back through hundreds of years. People had been here, stored things here, kept fuel, bottles, chests of drawers, planks with whitewash on them, wheels from clumsy pre-Victorian toys, toys themselves, a hobby-horse, a warped blackboard, garden tools.

'A right tip,' said Frank, crushing his way across books bound in leather, scraping his boot to the floor. 'Safe enough. Where's the light from?'

'From the wall at the back,' said Keith. He had a sentence ready in his mind, and swallowed it without mouthing it first – I didn't see it before, because it was a sunny day. He would not be able to explain the utterance.

'You're right about the cellar,' said Frank. 'It's a tidy spot.' He meant it would be useful, not that it was orderly or neat. 'Now get thysen right about the lease document, Keith.'

It had been a harder journey than Keith expected, having to overcome the obstacle of a non-existent cellar, and the scornful hostility of Frank.

'Simple,' he said, knowing exactly where the document was, high up behind a carefully placed stone in the rough cliff of the back wall.

Upstairs Dr Tate stamped again and showered the cellar with grit from the underside of the flags and the stone beams that held them up.

Keith navigated round the wreck of a wheelbarrow and the cast-iron base of a school desk, and got to the back wall.

Light came out through cracks and joints in the natural stone, cold and steady, a pervasive luminosity, a cave full of it.

Keith looked for the place where he had pushed in the concealing stone to hide the parchment.

The stone was still there, unwilling to come out. For a moment he thought he was mistaken and it was part of the rock. But Nellie Jack John's hand came over his shoulder and lifted it away.

'Owt?' he said.

'Nowt,' said Keith. Nellie Jack John dropped the stone.

Keith reached into the hole. There was another stone. He handed it out, said, 'Nowt' again. and Nellie Jack John dropped it too; and the same with the third.

Keith had put three stones in after the parchment. There should not have been a fourth, but there was, and he had to say 'Nowt' again, and the same for the fifth stone, with his arm reaching in to the structured back of the hole.

There were cobwebs. There was a spider running on his fingers, glittering as he dropped it at Nellie Jack John's feet. Nellie Jack John would have crushed it with his boot, but it scuttled flashily away, bright and quick.

Beside the cobwebs something moved. He brought out a swollen gross cylinder that once (last September only, a century or two ago) had been an aluminium torch.

'Ket,' said Nellie Jack John, and dropped it on the floor.

The next thing had survived most of its decay, but the red plastic had been degraded, and the stainless steel had become pitted as if the Swiss Army knife had been boiled in stronger acids than time. Keith slipped that into his own pocket.

There was a little stack of cold coins, green or black with age.

'Them's spent up,' said Nellie Jack John.

'Is it there?' asked Frank. 'This lease?'

There was nothing more in the hole but a disk of reddish shale. Keith held it, and looked at Frank.

Frank put his arm in the hole. He brought out spider web, and that was all. There was a silence as many hands each felt in turn for other loose stones and cavities behind them, but there was nothing ready to move..

'It's not here,' said Keith. 'Frank, it's not here. But . . . ' He could say no more. He could not explain that he had put the deed here, the stone, the coin. No one believed he had put anything there at all. Yet he had found the cellar that could not exist.

'There's summat,' said Frank, at the back kitchen sink, foam from yellow soap to the elbows.

'And nowt,' said Sally, who was busily drying Nellie Jack

John's arms, because she said he was no good at manning for himself.

Keith went back into the farm kitchen. The fire flicked, and a puff of smoke bellied out into the room. Alec-Edward drank a cup of hot tea and his eyes popped wide open.

'Keith,' said David, not understanding how Keith could behave in such a way.

'I'll look again,' said Keith, hopelessly.

'I'll put the wall back,' said Frank. 'And plaster over. There's nowt else to do. We'll leave the place right for the next folk, if we can't get a lease, and if they want a tidy cellar they can have it. That's that, Keith. We'll maybe say nowt to your father, when he lands. It would trouble him to learn of it.'

EIGHT

Mr Heseltine was in the room, coming in quietly when no one was looking, making the fire smoke, closing the door behind him, rubbing wet Gytrash pawmarks off his coat.

'Now, Frank,' he said, seeing everybody standing about in tension, Eileen pouring tea with two trembling hands. 'What is it?'

'Oh, Mr Heseltine,' said Frank, straightaway 'here's Keith said the deed, the lease, that thing, was in the cellar here, but shaff, there's nowt.'

'Cellar?' said Mr Heseltine. 'Have you a cellar?'

'Keith found it,' said Frank. 'For us. But the paper wasn't in it. There was nowt.'

'The deed,' said Keith. 'The lease document, the indenture. It wasn't there.'

'No,' said Mr Heseltine. He waited for sense to be spoken.

Only David had found anything of interest, and handled the red stone disc, hearing it sing as he rubbed it, hearing the pieces in his pocket respond. But for the moment he said nothing, in spite of a certain clear idea that no longer was complete nonsense.

'Deed, Keith?' said Mr Heseltine, hearing no sense from anyone, stepping forward and putting a leather bag on the table. He had to move a plate nearer Alec-Edward to do so. Alec-Edward accepted the invitation to a cheese slice. 'How can the deed be there, Keith? Of course it isn't in a cellar here, especially if there isn't a cellar. How could you think such a thing? I've just come from the Land Deeds Registry, where they've been trying to find it for months, and today I stood over them myself until they did. It's been there thirty years and more, since my father's time, when it went to be safer than in our office. I have it here.'

He clicked back the two catches of the bag, and pulled the top open.

'I've had a quick look at it, and everything is clear. I'll just explain, Frank, that you won't be getting a new lease.'

'Well, we wondered,' said Frank, all dismay. 'That sets Keith in a cruel light, only that he was doing his best.'

'No,' said Keith. 'I knew, I knew.'

'Nonsense,' said Mr Heseltine.

Eileen was sobbing by the fire, putting the teapot on the fire and the kettle on the table. Kirstie rushed to rescue those things, Lyddy went to comfort her. But she's also ingratiating herself with her mother, thought David.

'No more lease,' said Mr Heseltine. 'I could criticise the wording of the deed, considered in modern terms it's shakily written (I suppose that in those days they had to article members of the family), but we looked at it in the Registry, and I've put in a provisional re-registration for the owner, who is the beneficiary the house and farm will come to at the end of the present lease.'

'Today,' said Eileen. 'This is the last day.'

'Yesterday,' said Mr Heseltine. 'You didn't pay yesterday, Frank, and the lease ran out at midnight.'

'I hope I can get alongside the new owner,' said Frank. He was continuing to say, 'And work summat out,' but Mr Heseltine spoke over him.

'Get alongside the new owner, Frank? You won't manage that, lad.'

'I'll just sit down a minute,' said Frank. 'Are you sure, sir?'

'You can't get alongside yourself,' said Mr Heseltine. 'This deed states that the tenant at the end of the lease, of almost two hundred and fifty years, is the beneficiary. Swang Farm belongs to you, Frank. It's yours. You are the owner.'

'No more rent?' said Frank. 'But I'll miss paying it, that I will.'

'Ours,' said Eileen, and Kirstie held her because she sagged where she stood.

'There's more,' said Mr Heseltine. 'There's things Keith doesn't know.'

'He doesn't know much,' said Frank. 'What ailed you, Keith, to go the way you did? Finding that shaffling cellar full of ket.'

Kirstie deposited Eileen in a chair. She was not faint, but overcome with relief. 'Eh, look at the tablecloth,' she said. 'I put the kettle on it.'

'No rent to pay?' said David, who had been putting together pieces of stone at the other end of the table, putting them together so that they almost stayed put. 'Is this the rent cup?'

Keith said, 'How did you know?' and dug in his pocket for something. 'I never showed it to you.'

He brought out a red wax seal, with a broken tag of worn ribbon on it. 'That's it, that's the rent cup.' On the seal was a shape that David had formed with the stones.

'Just a top bit missing,' said Keith. 'A sort of spike.'

'But I don't have to pay it,' said Frank. 'I won't belong to anything, not be part of it, oh dear.'

Over by the fire Lyddy was beginning to find her tongue and fight back at Kirstie. 'No I will not go home,' she said. 'I don't want to be at home with you, I've given you up, I am going back with Alec-Edward, and I am giving up your house, and when I am as old as you I will come back and tell you what to do. I am not going to stay. I'm giving everything back and I wish I wasn't christened because they don't do that where I'm going.'

She was digging in her school bag and scattering objects on the floor and on the table, vests, pencils, toys, knickers, two red plastic dolls' cups, My Little Pony, a yelping Cyberpet ('It needs feeding, someone,') and, loudest of all when she threw it, the eight-faced crystal Nellie Jack John had given her at her own christening. It bounced clear over a plate of jam tarts and rolled on its four central sides and angles to David. It lay almost transparent, with a centre that might be moving, its shadow on the cloth almost alive.

'Aye,' said Nellie Jack John.

'What is that?' said Dr Tate. 'I don't know that stone, or any of those, Wix. What are they?'

'Artificial,' said David, because he knew, because the threads of thought in his mind were alive again, because . . .

'It's just that,' said Nellie Jack John, 'it goes on top of that, David, and it'll ho'd togither.'

David was finding that. The octahedron at the top and the disc at the bottom held the thin flakes of stone together, and the rent cup was complete, luminous in his hands.

'Let me hold it,' said Lyddy. 'Some of it is mine.'

It was not only the rent cup. Something bright walked across the table on its many legs, and into the hollow inside of the cup, reached up its legs, and pulled the crystal down on top of it. Something that needed it, that had needed it and longed for it for many centuries. And from David's point of view, the last score and a half of months, while he did not understand what had to be done.

'Money-spider,' said Lyddy.

David was speechless, but he knew that the inevitable right thing had happened, that this tiny thing had approached and entered his mind, and had been trying to make him find and assemble the cup, because it was the jar that held the elements from the beginning of time.

'Chrono-leptons,' said David.

'Chrono-leptons,' said Dr Tate, watching, but at the same time reading the deed the other side of the table, under the still-swaying overhead light.

David withdrew his hands from the cup, because it was making them stand away, buzzing and repelling and tingling.

Lyddy put her hands there instead, relishing the sensation,

showing her teeth, where she felt it most.

The cup began to change. Its separate parts blended together and changed their dimensions and shape. The blending, or joining, substance was a buzzing growth of silk, spider silk, stitching and pasting the stones together like the web on a house-leek.

'Arran-web,' said Nellie Jack John. 'It's him inside siling that out.'

The lower part became like a cylinder, sewn white as wax. The crystal at the top began to glow, and turn like flame. For some short moments, as they all watched, the candle that Nellie Jack John had brought out of the hill stood on the table before them.

It was no more than a candle in size, with a flame like an almond. But its weight made the table creak in its joints, and the wood splinter beneath the sudden inordinate weight. Lyddy pulled her hands away, but still held on.

'It meant to do it,' she said.

Outside, in the rain, bugles and trumpets were sounding, in an added, unexpected, and confusing noise.

'By God,' said Nellie Jack John, 'get up at the attention, parade time; I ken that racket.' But then he knew he was no longer a soldier, and looked round.

Before he could speak again a drum began beating outside the house, tunk, tunk, tunk, approaching, tunk-a-tunk, standing still at the front door.

'Now what?' said Eileen. 'It's enough without that. What is it?'

The front door began to shake under the heavy fist of someone demanding admittance.

'Them Scotch boogers,' said Nellie Jack John, nodding his head in understanding. 'We're good as dead.'

Eileen hooted with dismay. Alec-Edward belched. Sally clung to Nellie Jack John. The house continued to echo to the summons at the door. The bugles sounded forth again.

NINE

'The daft lile beggar,' said Nellie Jack John, with a big grin. He knew what was happening. He went out of the room, along the passage covered in fallen stone, kicked rubble away from the front door, and pulled it open.

'It's a lot wetter than we hoped,' said Captain Chapman. This time he was in uniform, streaked with rain. Beside him a regimental drummer rapped out a brisk tattoo on a drum.

Ten paces away Jip was standing tall, his lips back in a snarl, his ears flat, his nose sensing what was on the air.

The drummer was wearing a bright uniform, cleaner than Nellie Jack John had ever seen it, mended and complete.

'Is that my size?' said Nellie Jack John, stepping forward and adjusting a strap, a button, the belt that held the drum. 'I were a lile lad then.'

'Cover the drum,' Captain Chapman told the drummer. 'Keep the head dry.'

'It's not paper,' said Nellie Jack John. 'It won't hurt. It lived wild afore I catched it. Will-ta come in and sup tea, or summat, take a bite to eat? Mother!'

'I see you have visitors already,' said Captain Chapman.

'They're not company,' said Nellie Jack John. 'Some on 'em is family, and the rest lawyers, and we've finished all our business.'

Captain Chapman shook his head. 'We just came up to make a bit of noise for you,' he said, 'to show you the new drum head in place. And to ask you what kind of skin it is, because we can't find a match for it in all the parchment we know.'

'It's Attercop,' said Nellie Jack John. 'I kepped Attercop, and he nigh got me and all.' He rubbed his hand along the edge of his chin, where the skin was burnt and wrinkled. 'Teng'd me, the lile moor-booger, so I cured his skin. Bray him ivery day, put two men on t'job, and pay him back.'

Captain Chapman did not believe there was such a creature. He saluted. 'About turn, quick march. Drummer. Bugles.'

'Daft devils,' said Nellie Jack John. 'Get away by, Jip, t'moor-booger's dead.'

He closed the door on the noise that was beginning again outside. His wrists were flicking in time to the drum, and his foot tapping to the sound of the bugle. 'It were worth it.'

The soldiers had a Land Rover in front of the house. They reached it, watched from the window of the kitchen, and from the front door, where David had pulled it open again, thinking that Nellie Jack John's manners were still rough and always would be, closing it on his friendly visitors.

'It's still ramm,' said Nellie Jack John, sniffing for the scent of Attercop. 'They'll always know it for Attercop leather.'

Then men marked time, turned round, and the drum rattled for a fanfare to begin. Jip held back, glad to see his enemy Attercop going.

'It's what the duke gets,' said Nellie Jack John. 'They must be right plea . . .'

The house shook under his feet and his word did not end. The fanfare outside crashed into discord and shouts. The drum stopped in mid roll. A sound like earthquake, like the falling of giant weights, began round the house, stroke after stroke, now to one side, now to the other, as if they were bracketing the house and the final blow on the roof itself, the noise stopped. The floors stood still. Dust that hung in the air began to settle.

Lyddy was on the floor, wringing her hands, where something had moved and stung them, like a vast slap. 'I've dropped it,' she said. But she had dropped nothing. Something in the house had dropped her.

Following the great noises outside, the candle between her hands had changed again. With a gentle but percussive thud or puff it had left local time, and the space it had filled collapsed like a vacuum, imploding and jolting everyone and everything in the room, more closely and nearly than what had happened outside. Overhead the boggarts grumbled, and settled to sleep again.

David brushed away from his face the thought that wings might have touched it, like light in his eyes, colour across his mind, and something like the scars of migraine transient in his eyes.

Lyddy did not cry, or snivel, or sob, but the tears flowed down her face and darkened her sweatshirt. 'You didn't need to do that, Davy,' she said, getting up cautiously. 'You only had to be nice to me.'

David shook his head. He had done nothing. Lyddy looked out of the window.

Alec-Edward took a chocolate wafer biscuit, dipped it in salad dressing, and began to lick it. Everybody else stared from face to face.

'Locked in,' said Lyddy. 'We're locked in. The soldiers are coming back.'

The front door was banged again.

'What have they done?' said Eileen. 'They shouldn't have.'

'They can't get out,' said Lyddy.

'Theophany,' said Sally.

'God,' said Keith, sure that a visitation would fall on him for forgery and misrepresentation.

'Cosmology,' said Dr Tate, who was looking from the window too. 'The GPS was right as well as wrong. Its batteries can't just be failing every time I bring it up here. But a place on the surface appears to move, or several places seem to be the same one, and time is where the place is, fixed in time, and moving because of precession, disregarding our opinion of where things are on the surface of the planet. That would account for it.'

He was talking to himself.

Nellie Jack John was at the front door, pulling it open again. 'Is it the Scotch landed?' he asked.

A soldier stood there. 'Is there another road?' he said. 'We can't get our vehicle out. They'll blame me for this.' He held out a crushed bugle.

'I said so,' said Lyddy, running out into the rain to make sure of what she had seen.

The rest of the houseful followed her. The soldiers could not get their vehicle out from where it had been driven to the front of the house and parked beside Dr Tate's car.

Now, between them and the lane to Swang, a quadrant of the circle of Jingle Stones stood, encompassing the house, locking the cars in. It was their noise that had thundered like missiles as they were lodged into these fresh sites. Their weight had pounded and battered the ground, and the displaced air had pulsed and in waves.

'Longbows at Agincourt,' said Dr Tate.

At the back of the house dark sentinels paraded across the yard. Here, as well, they locked in the tractor, Mr Heseltine's car, Frank's Land Rover, David's, and all the farm equipment waiting to be used on the hayfields.

'Clamped,' said Frank. 'T'house is clamped.'

'I never saw anything like it,' said Mr Heseltine. 'It's inexplicable.'

'But it explains,' said Dr Tate. 'It explains why I never got a GPS reading between here and the Jingle Stones. The instrument always said they were the same place, and I always thought it was the battery running down. The explanation is much simpler, though contrary to reason, or at least probability. Precession.'

'They're the same spot,' said Nellie Jack John. 'Just moved apart across time. I've been in yon cellar when it was part lead mine and up on t'hill.'

'Geology,' said David.

'I've heard stuff moving below,' said Eileen,

'It was all one event,' said Dr Tate. 'This candle thing, Heseltine, Wix, all tied up with Jingle Stones, at the centre of them all.'

Keith was pacing about. 'I reckon,' he said, 'that the middle of the circle is just at the middle of the kitchen, where the candle was.'

'Is the telephone still working?' asked Captain Chapman. 'We'd better call the lads up here and get our vehicle out. Strange our driver didn't see them when we came in.'

During the rest of the midsummer evening, into the bright following night, they lifted all the vehicles out with a high jib, and set them on the lane. The men were happy to leave.

'They're complaining of invisible animals,' said Captain Chapman, having his third cup of tea. 'Playing under their feet.'

'Cats,' said Lyddy, yawning.

'She always thinks they are cats,' said Eileen. 'It's just the boggarts. They got shaken out. They like it. Now they feel at home. They were never content in the house, always uneasy. They feel safe with a fence round them again. It's what it's for, after all.'

Men were being teased by boggarts. Boggarts were swinging on the jib and running underfoot. Gytrash was taking deep breaths and trying to smell them, or squinting hugely and pretending to see them, while they were pulling his tail. Jip snapped if they came near, and now and then cast a growl towards the drum.

'Boggarts?' said Captain Chapman. 'I can't tell the lads that.

I'll tell them it's rock-lag and they'll get over it. The M.O. will give them an injection tomorrow, and that cures most things.'

TEN

'Keith,' said Dr Tate, later on, but before the army had gone, and Alec-Edward had been to sleep and woken again, and Lyddy was beginning to whine. 'What made you think the deed was in an imaginary cellar that turned out to exist?'

'Instinct,' said Keith. 'Not much of one.'

'I don't know,' said Dr Tate. 'Did you put it there?'

'He can't have done,' said Mr Heseltine. 'It was in the Registry a dozen years before he was born, lost in the files.'

'I see here the date it was signed and set up,' said Dr Tate, in the voice that meant he was being clever. 'It never was.'

'But it's a valid document,' said Mr Heseltine. 'Who's going to dispute it?'

'I don't know,' said Dr Tate. 'It was signed on Friday the eleventh of September, 1752.'

'What about it?' said Keith. Something had begun to come into his mind, something that happened after the War of the Spanish Succession, a curiosity David had mentioned, but Keith had disregarded.

'There was no such day,' said Dr Tate. 'Wednesday the second of September 1752 was followed immediately by Thursday the fourteenth. There was no Friday between, there was no 11th of September. The calendar was being adjusted. People were very alarmed by that, and wanted their time back. They felt they'd lost wages, and so on, and there were riots.'

'Perhaps,' said Keith, feeling for some remark that showed how wise he had been.

'But it can't be anything to do with you?' said Dr Tate. 'Can it?'

'It's impossible,' said Mr Heseltine.

'I accept that,' said Dr Tate. 'But it's something Keith would have missed, leaving school in the middle of that period of history. I told you I was here as a historian.'

'You've proved that,' said Dr Wix. 'But nothing else.'

Alec-Edward found room for a butterfly bun, dipped wing by wing in salad dressing.

'Nothing else?' said Dr Tate. 'Nothing else, Keith?'

Keith stayed quiet. The business was all done now. There was no more to say.

Everybody looked at Keith again. This time he had nothing to support him. He blushed, he felt himself turning red all over, heat radiating from him.

'I don't know anything about dates,' he said, because his blushing had found him out, he was being looked at, and had to respond.

'He borrowed my ink and a feather,' said Lyddy. 'He put it up his nose and sneezed.'

'Shut up,' said Keith, thinking that little girls know things by instinct, not by fact; such things as Keith having a fraudulent lie on his conscience.

'Before Keith and I go,' said Mr Heseltine, getting a book from his bag, '– for breakfast – there's one more little item. Keith doesn't know about it, so he can't have got it wrong. For all the time the lease has run, two hundred and forty-seven years odd, the rents, which amounted to the profit on half a dozen lambs, have gone into an account, which built up a certain amount of capital. That money has been invested by our firm as trustees, and now the lease is ended, that money also goes to the owner of Swang Farm Estates.'

'That's nice,' said Eileen. 'Thoughtful.'

'It'll be a few hundred,' said Frank. 'Over the years.'

'And welcome,' said Eileen. 'A new bath, maybe.'

'Yes,' said Mr Heseltine. 'Something of the sort. You could have gold taps. With the tax paid, it comes to slightly over a quarter of a million pounds.'

This time Eileen overwhelmingly slid from her chair to the floor. Dr Wix attended to her, and nurse Kirstie stood by her.

'Always have a medical team in attendance,' said Dr Wix. 'Good luck can be so stressful.'

'Well,' said Eileen. 'I never heard anyone say so much money at once in my house. It gave me a turn.'

'Money-spider,' said Lyddy. 'I knew.'

When the world was quiet outside they heard the Jingle Stones sing and settle themselves into place, shifting in the soil until

216

they were happy. David stroked and tapped them, and the resulting resonance went round the circle like a conversation.

'They never got used to being up yonder,' said Frank. 'I reckon.'

'Home,' said Eileen.

Alec-Edward could not return home.

'My uncle wi' a name like it,' said Nellie Jack John, 'before my time, like, got hissel' lost when he were sike a lile lad, and this is him, belike. He'd better stop down wi'us and learn the job. We'll have someone to take over when all's said and done.'

He could not go back, because nowhere between the Jingle Stones, in the summer twilight before dawn, was there a way through for Nellie Jack John to lead him to his own time.

'I can make nowt of it,' he said. 'I isn't getting thruff to anywhere. It's the same all sides. It's stopped being yonder; it's all this side of the spot. We can't get t'lile lad back, and he can't get hisself back. He'll have to stop at Swang. There's eneugh to go round, and Sally doesn't mind a family ready begun.'

'I'll get him some bath salts,' said Sally. 'When we get that bath. He's the eldest one, so far.'

'Keep him for me,' said Lyddy. 'I shall need a farmer for my lambs. He's my property. But I really wanted a little devil with a tail.'

In September, after Lyddy had been unclasped from the bridegroom, Nellie Jack John ('I isn't off to France, sithee') and Sally ('It's sunshine, stupid') had left for the airport, Lyddy and

Gytrash slipped away with Alec-Edward from the remainder of the party and the hired juke box at Swang, taking sausage rolls and meringues, and half a bottle of what she called sneezing wine.

All three were found in the wrong 4WD at Whashton, where a guest had returned with them asleep in the back, thinking they were pigs, all snoring when asleep, and complaining of headaches when they woke.

'I'd a grand puke behind t'driver's chair,' said Alec-Edward.

Gytrash was laughing in a sinister way at strange dog jokes.

Nellie Jack John, back from Tenerife, said, 'Mother, make me a pie, I've had nowt solid i' weeks.'

Sally said, 'It's me he means for mother.'

'Sarah Cherry,' said Nellie Jack John. 'Missus, see-est-ta.'

'Siesta?' said Sally. 'Nowt but eat and sleep, thou!'

'You'll never keep up with Alec-Edward too,' said Eileen, when Sally had stopped laughing.

'I've got the pair of you,' said Alec-Edward, content about that.

Round Swang Farm the Jingle Stones stood content too, and boggarts roamed the garden inside, like pets.